Duck's Landing

A NEW ENGLAND SEACOAST ROMANCE

CAMERON D. GARRIEPY

Buck's Landing
Copyright © 2012 Cameron D. Garriepy
Bannerwing Books
All rights reserved.

Cover design by Bannerwing Cover Design, with photography courtesy of
Unsplash

Print Edition:
ISBN: 0615689777
ISBN-13: 978-0615689777

This book is respectfully dedicated to the residents of Hampton Beach, NH.

Please forgive me any liberties I have taken, and know that this story is written with the greatest affection for the beach, the boardwalk, and the community which makes Hampton so very special to my family.

Special Thanks

This book was made possible through the incredible generosity of a very special group of investors:

Judith G. Zamore
Elizabeth & Gary Brown ~ Rebecca DiJulia
Amy Lipke ~ Heather Sanborn
Nichole Beaudry ~ Roxane Bock
Kirsten Piccini
Veronique Corddin
John Batzer ~ Nancy Campbell
Elizabeth Goeke ~ Ari Gottlieb
Lex Marburger ~ Erin Best
Renee McKinley ~ Katherine O'Grady
Lori O'Hara ~ Frank Wildermann
Angela Amman ~ Phoebe Ramsey
Alta Dantzler ~ Marian Kent
Victoria Kirichok ~ Tara L. Lagana
Kelly Keen Dillon ~ Heather Young
Kath Galasso ~ Kate Sluiter

Acknowledgments

It takes a village to write a novel, and I am privileged to practice my craft in a particularly wonderful one. Heartfelt thanks to everyone in my writing community, including but not limited to:

My family, especially my wonderful husband and son, for putting up with my devotion to writing—especially when inspiration struck on our summer vacation!

The friends and readers, near and far, who've supported me over the last few years. I write for myself. I publish for you.

The enigmatic K, who is always right.

Mandy and Angela, for hours of critique. I hope I've done you proud.

Roxanne, my editrix extraordinaire, thank you for whipping the manuscript into shape with a professional eye.

My dear Write on Edge colleagues, I love you like sisters (yeah, you, too, John!).

What's in this book?

CONTENT INFORMATION

Dear Reader,

Buck's Landing *is a standalone small town romance with an HEA, set in a real coastal New Hampshire town (though many liberties have been taken). It contains open-door, sweet-with-heat sex scenes, occasional coarse language, alcohol consumption/an alcoholic parent/spouse, families with babies/young children, and dealing with the grief of a loved one. If any of these topics are sensitive, please read on with caution.*

Tropes/themes you'll find inside:

- *girl/boy next door*
- *badly behaved cat*
- *you can't go home again*
- *competence is sexy*
- *cinnamon roll hero*
- *H/h over 30*

Puck's Landing

One

Whoever was pounding on the door had better have their affairs in order, Sofia thought as she pushed herself up off the sofa, because she was going to murder them with her bare hands. With a grimace at the empty bottle of pinot noir on the coffee table, she cursed herself for drinking too much the night before, pressing her knuckles against her sleep-crusted eyes. Hadn't she fled this coastal New England beach town to escape her father's drinking? She scraped her mane of dark brown curls into a hasty knot, wondering what the hell else a lone woman was expected to do in Hampton Beach when she wasn't one of the vacationing hordes.

A glance at the clock told her she'd overslept. The mini-golf course at Buck's Landing would be open by now, and she should be getting the Snack Bar ready.

She opened the door to Amy, her assistant manager. The co-ed's perky ponytail and crisp uniform polo shirt practically sparkled in the July sun.

"I'm sorry, Sofia." Amy glanced down from Sofia's third

story landing at the Astroturf greens, where a small crowd had gathered around the cement "tree" on the twelfth hole. "There's a kitten stuck up the tree, and I can't get him down."

"Of course." With a sigh, Sofia slid her feet into the sensible sport sandals she wore to work, and followed Amy down the stairs to the waiting cat. She praised herself for falling asleep in a tank top and soft cotton pants. At least she was decent enough to rescue stray kittens from fake cement trees.

The sun glittered off the crushed stone paths that wound through the course, sparkled on the blue-gray sea washing ashore across the street at the state beach. Heat was already pooling on the sidewalk, the boardwalk, and the road between. Sofia squinted, wishing for sunglasses, and did her best to ignore the faint throbbing at her temple.

A six-foot ladder proved enough to get her into the tree, and the little scrap of fur came to her easily. Sofia had never had a cat, but as this kitten's body went soft in her hands, she wondered briefly why not.

"Aren't you a pretty...well, now what are you?" She raised the tiny cat up and inspected its underside. "A pretty boy." He cocked his head to one side, and Sofia chuckled. She tucked the purring feline under her arm and backed down the ladder. "Amy, can you stash the ladder on your way back to the window? I'm going to find a place for this guy to stay until I find his owner."

"Sure."

Sofia envied the college girl's boundless energy. She hadn't remembered having that much buoyant charm at twenty-two. All she remembered about being a college kid was planning her summers off from UNH so that she could be home as little as possible. The summer she was twenty-two, she'd worked her third consecutive summer at a girls' camp in the White Mountains, blessing them for providing room and board. She'd stashed her paychecks away, saving for the precious future, intent on escaping her father's grief and its companion, Canadian whiskey. She had planned to get out of New England, alone.

She carried the kitten up to the landing outside her apartment. Below her, Hampton's Ocean Boulevard was already awake and bustling. Salt and sand seasoned the breeze blowing in off the water. Motels, restaurants, food counters, and seaside souvenir shops lined the sidewalk of the boulevard as far as she could see before the coastline curved eastward at Rocky Bend. She smoothed out the cat's long tail while her eye traced the farthest point where the year-round colony sat on the bluff.

Buck's Landing sat amongst all the tourist traps, three stories high and half a block wide in every direction. Her grandfather had designed the mini-golf course on a parcel of land acquired after a fire, turning the charred remains of a boarding house into his personal dream of summer vacation family fun. Her father had run the course as a young man, bringing his new wife to live in the apartment on the third floor, turning the ground floor into an ice-cream and soda counter. It had been her mother who suggested, after Grampa Buck passed away, that they convert his second floor dwelling to apartments: weekly rentals for summer vacationers, monthly rentals for UNH students in the off-season.

While Sofia watched, the beach filled in with umbrellas and tents. Half a dozen kites flew over the boardwalk. Vacationing families were using the new bathhouse at the State Park—far better than the old one, she thought with a shudder. Kids and gulls shrieked from the high tide line, and the scent of Coppertone drifted over the piped-in music on the course. The kitten rested contentedly in the crook of her arm.

"You like it here, don't you?" She stroked one silky, steel gray ear. "You don't know that there's a whole world beyond this tacky town, a whole universe outside of New England."

The kitten's pleasant rumble was disturbed by the buzzing in her pocket. With her free hand, she fished out her phone. "Sofia Buck."

The tenants in 2B had clogged the toilet again. "I'll be right down."

Pocketing her phone, she shifted the small bundle on her arm. He blinked sleepily, stretching his skinny legs and flexing his fuzzy, half-dollar coin-sized paws.

"You're going to have to stay here alone for a few minutes. Can you do that?" Her companion yawned.

Sofia took him inside and carried him down the short hall, past the tiny bathroom and her parents' bedroom, to her childhood sanctuary. She focused on finding a pair of khaki shorts and a Buck's Landing polo, her glance coasting over the photos her father had set on the dresser sometime in the years between her departure and his death. There was a kind of madness in nostalgia, and Hampton Beach was not going to be her asylum.

Her guest began to knead the bedspread, and Sofia scooped him up. The kitten squeaked in protest. "No way, little man. This is the people bed, not the cat bed." She shut the bedroom door firmly behind her.

Plopping him down on the sofa, she headed for the utility closet. She grabbed a pair of long rubber gloves, a bucket, mop, and plunger. Giving the kitten a stern look, she said, "Be good."

She jogged down the stairs to the second of the two rental apartments that made up the second floor. This week, a family from upstate New York had 2B. During their brief exchange on Saturday afternoon, the mother had fretted over her.

"I'm so sorry to hear about your Dad, honey. He was such a nice man. Nick and I have been renting this place since before we got married. He was part of our vacation tradition."

Sofia had murmured the correct responses before showing them a few of the updates she'd arranged for over the past few weeks, including wireless internet. If she was going to be trapped in this place, she was at least going to be able to access the rest of the world from her laptop.

Pinning on her brightest smile, she knocked on the door. The mother opened the door. Her small child, a kindergartener named after a character from a movie—Trinity?—peered out from behind her legs.

"Hey, Sophie." The mother pushed a mop of sweaty curls from her forehead. "We're just heading across to the beach. Thanks for taking care of this."

Sofia swallowed the name correction that surfaced on her tongue. "Have fun. The waves are up this morning."

Thankfully, the toilet was only clogged with an abundance of quilted toilet paper. As she worked the plunger, she wondered what the fascination was with little kids and toilet paper rolls. Sofia cleaned up behind herself and locked the unit. She stowed the supplies back in her apartment, washed her hands, and poured herself a cup of coffee. Leaning on the counter to write up a to-do list, she ticked off her duties for the day.

The water in the fountain shared by the fourth and fifteenth holes was looking brackish, and she was running low on paper goods. Buck's Landing wasn't enough in the black to warrant a delivery service, which meant she'd be trucking over to Manchester for provisions and to stop at the pool supply place. And, at some point, she was going to have to call someone about the kitten.

She stood upright so quickly she nearly rapped her head on the upper cabinets. The kitten!

Her gaze flicked to the sofa, where a slight depression in her mother's once-favorite throw pillow was the only evidence of the feline adventurer's existence. She clicked her tongue and kissed the air in her apartment, willing the gray ball of fluff to appear from beneath some piece of furniture.

For twenty minutes she scoured her apartment for him, but the kitten was nowhere to be found. She was impressed. It was essentially a four room home. Her bedroom, the cramped-but-functional bathroom, her parents' bedroom, and the living space, with a single line of countertops and cabinets along one wall to hold the kitchen appliances. The dining table served as a visual separator for the room. When her efforts proved fruitless, she upped the ante, but a saucer of half-and-half and a bowl of chunk light tuna didn't coax the little monster out either. It wasn't until she went to the outside landing that she realized where he was.

The ghost of a smile played over her lips at the sight. Her furry friend had scaled another miniature landmark on the course. Not just any landmark, but the twelve-foot replica Easter Island head at the seventeenth hole.

Down again, out onto the course she went, grabbing the ladder from the utility room.

Amy spotted her coming. "He's awfully cute. Will you keep him?"

"I'm sure the little beast belongs to someone." Sofia propped the ladder against the statue and spoke to the three parties queued up at the tee. "Play through, folks. Amy will comp you all a soft-serve in the snack bar for your trouble." Amy herded everyone through while Sofia surveyed the head, looking for the best path to get to her little pal, who batted a passing white butterfly and mewed at her from his perch.

"WELL, I KNOW WHAT I'M GOING TO CALL YOU when I find you." Silas Wilde pushed up to standing, brushing a fine dusting of beach sand from his knees. He gave up hope that the little thing had only gone to ground under the sofa; he was fairly certain he was talking to an empty room. So far, the kitten his sister had given him at the beginning of the summer—a housewarming gift, or so Mallory claimed—had escaped his apartment no less than ten times, this last time managing, Silas feared, to get out of the building altogether.

He made a cursory examination of the bathroom and efficiency kitchen before taking the back stairway down to the Atlantis Market, the convenience store and gift shop that was his new livelihood, half-hoping the kitten was playing with the mops and brooms in the hallway. When his search disappointed him, he headed into the Market. His older sister's oldest son, Theo, looked up from the register. He was ringing up a big sale: two beach chairs, a soft-sided cooler, and a picnic's worth of bottled water, soda, and junk food.

Silas had developed a great affection for impulse beachgoers.

"Cat got out again," he said.

Theo laughed. "I've got everything taken care of."

Silas let himself out through the store's front door, leaving Theo to handle the morning beachcombers in search of a snow globe of the Casino Ballroom, a new pair of flip-flops, or aloe gel. "Hopefully, I won't be gone more than a half hour. I've got my phone."

Silas had traced the New England coast north from New York City six months earlier, abandoning Interstate 95 in Boston to weave a northbound route along route 1 and 1A, in a Jeep Wrangler he'd bought from the Want Ads. A thousand times, his breath was stolen by the pewter sea and the rocky shoreline, peppered with stretches of coarse sand beaches and faded boardwalks, but something about Hampton Beach called to him. Following the tug, he'd checked into a motel a block inland, one of the few open in the frigid winter months, and fallen asleep to the north wind wailing over the snowy beach.

He'd thought Ocean Boulevard had stolen his heart in January, abandoned and near silent, save for some hardy year-round dwellers and a handful of businesses that defied the off-season. As he looked out over the summer expanse of state beach, pristine and already baking under a ninety-degree sun, the music of tourism and the magic of vacation coursed through him like the first swallow of a cold beer.

Had he still been in New York, sweltering in his Brooklyn walk-up or hunched over his desk in the maze of cubicles on the litigation floor at Stern & Lowe, he might never have known the heady mix of kitsch and tradition that was Hampton. Owning a convenience store in a summer town was a good, long way from the document review sweatshop of corporate law.

Not even ten in the morning, and his worn R.E.M. tour tee-shirt was stuck to the small of his back. A bead of sweat rolled down his face, and he wiped it with the hem of the shirt. A gaggle of teenage girls wandered by in bikinis, and one of them turned to give him a sassy grin, her eyes lingering over the flat expanse of his stomach. Silas watched them pass, doing his best not to appreciate the view too much.

He walked the perimeter of his building, examining a patch of newer cedar shingles, not yet weathered silver, while he looked for the cat. The previous owner had taken care of the Atlantis, even if his taste in interior decorating was a blend of seventies aesthetic and thrift store pragmatism. Silas called to the kitten with the whistle and click combination he'd found seemed to attract the small adventurer.

It wasn't long before he heard the meow from over the fence. The kitten was small, but he had lungs and feet worth watching. Following the cries, he arrived at the gate of Buck's Landing. His next door neighbor's building was taller, casting his apartment into welcome shade for most of the day. The owner, Jimmy Buck, had passed away about a month ago, leaving the whole property to his estranged daughter.

The jury was still out on the new Buck at the Landing, as far as Silas was concerned. She'd breezed into town in a slick BMW sedan, holed up in her late father's apartment, and kept mostly to herself. He'd only seen her once in the three weeks she'd been in residence; she'd been hauling a huge suitcase out of the trunk of that Beamer. She had refused his friendly offer of help, called down over the railing from the porch roof that served as his deck. He'd watched Jimmy's daughter drag that luggage up the two flights of narrow exterior stairs to the apartment with equal parts amusement and distaste.

Silas recognized the young woman working the register

9

at Buck's. Amy had pounded pavement before the last frost looking for a summer job, even coming into the Atlantis Market to see if he was hiring. Turning her down had been tough, so he'd been glad to hear Jimmy had hired her on for the summer. Later in the spring when he'd run the numbers and knew he could afford a part-timer, he'd hired his nephew Theo at his sister's insistence. Mallory was a persistent woman.

"Amy." He smiled. She was reading one of those creased and worn steamy beach novels that passed from rental to rental. He imagined this one had been up and down the strip. Amy stashed the novel under the counter.

"Mr. Wilde. Can I help you?"

"I'm wondering if you've seen a kitten around the place this morning."

Amy lit up like the Funarama on a Saturday night. "Seventeenth hole. He's a troublemaker, huh?"

"You could say that. Thinking of calling him Houdini." He peered around the building towards the course. "Seventeen, you said?"

"Go on through, Mr. Wilde."

Silas couldn't help inspecting Jimmy Buck's Astroturf and the gravel paths that wound between the holes as he walked. Jimmy had been a good neighbor in the few months they'd known one another. The older man had introduced himself immediately following the first evening Silas spent in the apartment over the Atlantis; Jimmy had turned up on the welcome mat with a pair of to-go coffees and a half-dozen box of donuts. They'd grown close before his passing. Jimmy had told him stories about his family, mainly centered on his daughter's childhood, and had often confided in Silas that he wished he had more time and resources to put into the endless maintenance the property required.

There were changes at Buck's Landing, Silas noted. He had to admit, they were for the better. The paths were weeded, their gravel leveled. The turf and obstacles had been cleaned, and the greens patched in the worn spots. The music Jimmy had favored leaned toward classic country and western, so much so that Silas considered loaning the man his collection of Police and U2 CDs. Today he appreciated the thump of bass and electronic warble of Auto-Tune. The younger Buck knew what the kids listened to, anyway.

He heard Jimmy's daughter before she came into view. Unlike the over-produced pop-princess voice on the sound system, hers was a smoky voice that belonged in a speakeasy.

He rounded the corner at the sixteenth hole and burst out laughing. There was Houdini, surveying his kingdom from the top of the Easter Island head, his posture comically regal. The cat watched his would-be rescuer hoist herself from a short ladder by using the statue's left shoulder as a foothold.

"Come on, sweetheart," she cajoled, that bourbon voice pitched low. With an arm wrapped around the statue's head, she swung her leg over it, braced her other foot against its chest, and reached up for his cat.

Silas closed the distance between them and pushed his hair back with his sunglasses, the better to get an eye full of Jimmy Buck's mini-golf heiress. Silas took in the khaki shorts stretched across a toned rear and the strong, tanned legs, and briefly envied the statue, with his cement face pressed against that body.

"That's one lucky statue," he said with a chuckle. "I see you found my cat."

ARROGANT BASTARD. SOFIA'S CHEEKS WENT HOT at the thought of how she looked, clinging to the impassive face of the golf course obstacle. There was a click and whistle from the man, and the kitten flicked its ears. With a flash of gray fur and a scrabble of little nails, he streaked down from the monolith.

"I think his name is Houdini," the man laughed.

Sofia couldn't tell if he was laughing at his own joke, at the cat's name, or at her predicament.

She swung her leg towards the ladder. When she'd taken a leave from her position as the event planner for the DeVarona hotel in Washington, DC, to return to Hampton Beach and sort out her father's property, she'd expected a hot, miserable summer of tourists in cheap tee-shirts spilling ice cream all over the run-down course. She hadn't been prepared for the changes to the old boulevard and the changes to Buck's Landing. She hadn't been prepared to get caught halfway up a Polynesian deity's face by her surfer-boy next door neighbor, but she was accustomed to damage control. She could face some local guy who'd lost his cat. When her foot missed and kicked the ladder instead of landing on a rung, she swore roundly and hung on to the cement.

To her horror, a pair of male hands steadied her, holding the backs of her thighs. The cheery conversations from the parties playing the course were gone, replaced by giggles and whispering.

"Easy now. I've got you." Her rescuer grasped her waist and lowered her to the turf. She sucked in a breath. It wouldn't do to fly off the handle in front of paying customers. Spinning around, she got a good look at her next door neighbor.

"You must be Jimmy's daughter," he said. The little gray cat sat on his broad shoulder like a pirate's parrot, delicately grooming one of his white-stockinged paws. "Thanks for helping out this little troublemaker. I'm Silas Wilde, your—"

"Next door neighbor, yes." She leveled him with her coolest managerial look and held out a hand. "Sofia Buck." His hands were big, she thought, watching hers disappear into his grip. And warm. His smile wrinkled his eyes, but she judged him to be near her age. From his shoulder, the kitten offered her his freshly groomed foot. His serious, whiskered expression charmed. "And you're Houdini."

Silas reached up and plucked the cat off his shoulder. "He's new, still getting the hang of being neighborly."

"I'd suggest locking your door, but he got out of my locked apartment earlier." She flicked an eyebrow at the pair. The gray kitten fit in his hand like a toy. "He's already been up the tree at hole twelve this morning."

Silas laughed, taking the measure of the so-called tree. Turning the kitten around to face him, he went nose-to-nose with his feline. "No more causing trouble for Ms. Buck. Though she does look fantastic stretched out on the moai."

Sofia snorted. "I am standing right here."

Silas turned his gaze on her. His eyes were the exact cool blue-gray of the Atlantic and his messy, honey-colored waves, pushed away from his face by a pair of sport sunglasses, were streaked summery blond. She felt his appraisal sweep over her. "So you are."

"Excuse me?" A barrel-chested man in a Red Sox tee-shirt was tapping his putter on the gravel. "Can we play?"

Sofia suppressed a grin as the sunburnt woman at his side smacked his upper arm and shushed him under her breath. "Please. I was just clearing up a hazard on the hole." She turned to Silas. "Mr. Wilde?"

"Silas." He stepped off the turf, Houdini settled in the crook of his arm. "And I've got to get back to the store."

Sofia flashed a smile at the golfers. "Enjoy your game."

She followed Silas's retreating form toward the gate, indulging in the fantastic view of his ass in hibiscus patterned surf shorts. When he stopped short, she very nearly crashed into him.

"Sofia," he said. "Let Houdini and I buy you a drink tonight."

She blinked. "No." Her manners surfaced. "Thank you, but no."

He scratched the cat's chin. "You've made the lady angry, you monster." His gaze was warm when he turned to her. "Another time, then."

ON HIS RETURN, SILAS HELPED A TRIO OF shirtless guys, swim-trunked and sandy, on their way into the Market. "Mornin', guys. Anything I can help you find?"

"You got Wiffle balls?" The leader cocked a grin at one of his buddies. "This loser knocked our last one into the ocean."

"Sure do." Silas pushed open the shop door. The loser in question was a blond kid who reminded him of himself not so very long ago.

The blond kid grinned. "I was distracted."

"Yeah, by the redhead in the string bikini," the apparent leader ribbed.

Silas exchanged a knowing glance with the guys. "Not such a bad distraction."

The vintage sign outside Buck's Landing caught his eye as the trio hurried out the door. Unbidden, the feel of Sofia Buck's muscled legs in his hands crept into his thoughts. Not such a bad distraction. Another time, for certain.

Two

Sofia had heard other people talk about high school reunions, about how seeing old friends after so long is shocking, how time makes alterations. She'd also heard it said that memory adjusts to accept the new version, and the years melt away.

The Judy who sat across from her at The Sandpiper Grill was three children softer than the lithe, bikini-wearing fawn she'd been in high school, but her eyes still sparkled, ready for the next big adventure.

"Sof, I can't believe you're here," she gushed, flipping her menu closed. "I mean, except for a couple of stops in town during college, I haven't seen you since that last bonfire on the beach."

Sofia couldn't argue, but unwelcome guilt pinched her conscience. She and her best friend had reconnected online a few years ago, but while Judy's profile shared everything from her kids' photos to the antics of the family dog, Sofia's reflected mostly her travel and professional friends from recent years. She hadn't even publicly mentioned her return to Hampton Beach. Judy, gambling that her father's death would bring Sofia to town, had left a note at the funeral home, urging her to call.

"What's good?" Sofia asked brightly, perusing the menu.

"Oh, I get the same thing every time. The Vietnamese Noodle Salad." Judy slid hers to the edge of the table. "Why didn't you ever come home?"

"Do you really have to ask, Jude?" Sofia sipped her water.

Judy's smile faltered.

"I didn't mean it like that."

"I think I always thought your dad would make it up to you."

Sofia smiled wistfully. Her optimistic friend was still the same. "Well, he didn't." She set her menu down with Judy's. "But if I'm stuck here for a few weeks, at least I get to see you again."

Judy reached across the table and squeezed her friend's hand.

"So," Sofia began, "tell me everything."

She leaned back in her seat and let the pleasure of Judy's company wash over her. Judy had married her college boyfriend right out of school. She had taught third grade for five years; he went to work for the family auto repair business. Then she'd gotten pregnant. Three kids and another five years later, she was getting ready to send her oldest to kindergarten.

"Nothing exciting, really, since Jake was born," she said. "Unless you count working most of the baby weight off this time." She giggled and gave her impressive cleavage a little squeeze. "Except these."

"Those," Sofia noted, "are exceptional."

"Enough about my boobs and my boring life. I want to hear about being fabulous in Washington."

Sofia toyed with her flatware before responding. "Fabulous? I don't know. It's good, though. I bought a place two years ago, a condo in Columbia Heights, and I'm managing the event staff now, which means my next career move might take me to a higher end market. DeVarona owns the Luxelle chain in Europe, and I've applied to one of the European properties."

"Oh my god," Judy gasped. "Like a Greek island? Or the south of France?"

"Got it on your first guess. Santorini."

"I don't know where that is," Judy sighed, "but it sounds like I want to go there."

Sofia grinned. "Once I've got the job, I'll bring you and Chris over for a second honeymoon."

Judy snorted. "Try a first. We took a long weekend in Bar Harbor, then Christopher had just started managing the garage, and I had spelling tests to grade."

Sofia raised her glass. "To a real honeymoon, then."

"You've come so far," Judy giggled, offering her own glass up. "Since the days of organizing beach parties."

Their glasses clinked, and a memory surfaced of her, Judy, and a couple dozen kids they knew driving up to one of the smaller beaches to have one of many illegal bonfires. She'd loved figuring out how to pull it off, down to arranging drivers and riders so they could hide their cars away from police notice.

Their waitress stopped by to take their order.

With their lunches ordered, Judy picked up the thread of conversation. "I guess it makes sense, you doing what you do. You were doing it even then."

"I was just thinking about that," Sofia admitted. "I've

19

never really looked at it like that before."

"Maybe the old Brain Twin powers are still there?" Judy touched her temple. "Just dormant until we were together again."

"I think so." Sofia said with a nod.

Judy waggled her eyebrows. "Does that mean I can use my influence to make you give up on Europe and stay here?"

"I can barely handle things as they are," Sofia said. "It's me, a college student, and a couple of teenagers. I don't know how my father managed it, honestly."

Judy took a deep breath. "I know you don't want to hear it, but he worked his ass off, Sof." She set her hands down flat on the table. "My Christopher is an alcoholic. Recovering. He knew your dad from AA. Jimmy's passing hit him hard. Your dad crawled out of the bottle, but he knew how bad he screwed up with you. He felt like leaving you alone was his penance, and nothing Christopher said could convince him otherwise."

Sofia heard the criticism in her friend's words. Judy didn't let up.

"He pulled Buck's Landing back from the edge, too. He almost lost it. That's what sent him looking for help. He didn't want to lose your Grandpa's property. He spent one whole winter getting sober and persuading the bank to give him a chance. Anywhere but here, that wouldn't have flown, but people still give a shit here, you know?"

"Yeah." Sofia was at a loss.

The arrival of their lunch diffused the moment.

"I'm sorry." Judy tossed the noodles in her salad. "I don't want to fight. It was just hard, knowing how badly he wanted to make things right, and how proud you both are, and then—"

"And then he died," Sofia said, spearing a bite of rare steak from her plate. She pushed a spinach leaf and some chèvre on to her fork, but couldn't bring herself to eat. Her stomach clenched. "And I have to live with that."

"Oh!" Judy looked stricken. "I'm a jerk. So much for a happy reunion."

"Judy," Sofia said. "Stop. You're just being honest with me. I used to love that about you. You always gave it to me straight."

Judy set her knife down. "I missed you."

"I missed you, too."

"Okay." Judy shifted the conversation. "So, you have a lair. Somewhere called Columbia Heights. Anyone you drag there regularly?"

Sofia nearly choked on half of a baby beet. "No. I'm not seeing anyone right now. Not regularly, anyway."

Judy's attention zeroed in. "There is someone."

"Seriously," Sofia said, "it's not a thing. There's a guy I've gone on a couple of dates with since the fall. He travels, though. Really." She pursed her lips. "It's not a thing."

"He travels enough that you've only gone out with him a couple times in three seasons?" Judy chewed contemplatively. "Is he a spy?"

"No." No, he's not, she thought. "He does...um... personal security."

"Is he good looking?"

"Yeah. Kind of weathered and tough."

Judy sighed happily. "I need someone to live vicariously through. Tell me a story about him."

"I met him at the bar of this fantastic French bistrot. I didn't notice his earpiece, or the rest of the suits, when he came up and asked us if we could relocate. I was awful to him; I tossed my hair and told him he needed to work on his pick-up lines." Sofia smiled at the memory. "And he flashes a badge and says, 'Ma'am, I'm going to have ask you to move. Now.'"

"Oh, my god!" Judy squealed. "Secret Service?"

Sofia nodded. "My friend and I got a table, had a few more drinks with dinner, and by the end of the night I was convinced I had to apologize. He was clearly still on duty, so I asked our waiter to slip him my card. I wrote 'I'm sorry I was rude,' on the back, and we ran outside, giggling, to hail a cab."

Judy burst out laughing. "And he called?"

"He did."

The rest of lunch passed easily enough. Judy was full of stories of their old friends, some still in the area, some scattered. Sofia loved the telling. Judy's humor and ease with the memory of their shared youth put a shine on each dramatic tale of cheating boyfriends, scandals, births and marriages, crimes and secrets.

Judy protested when Sofia took care of the check, but Sofia was adamant.

"Tell me you can take another hour," Judy said, wrapping up her stories. "I've got my sitter until three and I desperately need a pedicure."

Amy could handle the Landing for another hour. Sofia collected her purse. "Where to?"

"Oh, yay!" Judy clapped. "There's a cheap little place in the Walmart strip mall that does paraffin for thirty-five bucks."

Sofia hummed in anticipation. "You had me at paraffin."

SILAS HATED STRIP MALLS, BUT THEY WERE A necessary evil. Houdini had a serious catnip addiction, and in their short time together, he found that he was expected to provide a steady stream of burlap mice for the small assassin to eviscerate. The upside to his kitten's vicious appetite was that the little pain in the ass stayed at home if he was busy stalking herb-stuffed prey.

He hopped out of the Jeep and headed for the pet store. Two women were walking ahead of him, and he indulged in the sidewalk-devouring stride of the shorter, dark-haired woman. Her swishy skirt flirted with lean, strong calves, and shampoo-commercial curls bounced against her back.

The taller woman fluffed a perky blond ponytail, and turned to open the door to Nailz Plus, which boasted a "spa pedicure," whatever that was, for ONLY $35. She was softer through the hips, Silas noted, but stacked. Some days, he thought, being alive in the world was a beautiful thing. The brunette turned as well, and his lecherous thoughts kicked into overdrive.

Sofia Buck. He should have known that rearview. He jogged ahead and took the door from Sofia's companion. "Ladies."

"Thank you." The ponytailed friend had a million-watt smile.

"Silas." Sofia nodded.

Her friend stuck out a hand. "Judy Dunaway. I went to high school with Sofia. You know," she grinned, "last year."

"You're not both seniors?" He laughed. "Sofia had me convinced."

Judy's answering laugh was bell-like and musical. He liked her immediately. "Silas Wilde, proud owner of the Atlantis Market."

"Oh, perfect," Judy said. "You're neighbors!"

"That we are," he replied. "I'll let you two get to your pampering. Judy, it was a pleasure. Sofia, I'm sure I'll see you around."

"I'm sure," Sofia said, and followed her friend inside. Regally, he thought.

He tipped an imaginary hat as they entered the salon. The chemical-and-air freshener scent that whooshed out behind them stung his eyes.

As he headed for the pet store, he wondered idly if Sofia's friend was related to the Chris Dunaway who fixed his Jeep. His thoughts wandered to Sofia. She was so aloof, but there was something vital and warm about her. He filled a shopping basket with a wide variety of catnip toys. He understood his cat's obsession. He found he wanted to get past Sofia's tough outside, was convinced the good stuff was there under the surface.

Shaking his head at his own train of thought, he paid for Houdini's treats and headed to the Jeep.

———

"SILAS WILDE, HMM?" JUDY DROPPED HER FEET into the soaking tub and fiddled with the remote for her massage chair.

"Arrogant," Sofia said, fishing in her bag for a ponytail holder. She wrapped her hair up into a messy bun. "I met him last week. He came by the Landing looking for his lost cat."

"He's got a cat?" Judy arched a brow. "He doesn't strike me as a cat guy."

"And yet," Sofia said lightly, "he has one. A gray kitten. Whom I rescued twice that day."

"Oh," Judy smiled softly. "A kitten. That's cute."

"Yes, well," Sofia said dryly. "He got a good look at my ass while I was attempting to get the thing down from the Easter Island head on the seventeenth hole, and the little monster just climbed down to go to Silas."

To the amusement of the nail tech, Judy broke into snorting laughter.

Sofia attempted a half-hearted glare. "I'm glad you're amused."

"Oh, yes." Judy regained her breath. "You up there trying to save the cat, and your hunky neighbor hauls up and the 'stuck' cat just helps himself down? Comic gold, old friend."

"You suck." Sofia flipped open a People magazine and pretended to sulk until Judy smacked her with Real Simple. "Ow!"

"So, is he single?" Judy apparently had a one-track mind.

Sofia peered over her magazine while the nail tech scrubbed her feet. "I have no idea."

Judy flipped open her phone's keyboard and started typing. Within a moment or two, text message pings started coming in. Judy giggled.

"What are you doing?" Sofia's heart sank. "Jude?"

"He's single. New in town. Drinks at The Salty Cod, plays darts with Chuck Kellogg and Marty Swanson when there's a game going. Generally considered hot."

"Generally?" Sofia couldn't help it.

"And I quote Meg Lafferty; you remember Meg? Um..." She squinted at her phone as if it held the answers. "She was Meg Carson? She works at the Town Clerk's office. She says, 'If you like that bed-head, surfer thing.'"

Both women laughed out loud.

"If?" Judy was chortling away again. She settled down

with an audible sigh, fixing onto Sophia the frightening matchmaking gaze of a happily married woman. "You should go out with him."

"Yes." Sofia snorted. "I'll just knock on his door and haul him off by his hair."

"Mmm. Yep." Judy dipped her feet into the warm water. "It's a mane, isn't it?"

"You're impossible. Were you always like this?"

Judy flashed her a grin. "I'm getting worse in my old age."

"Oh, god. Stop," Sofia moaned. "We're only thirty-two."

"Shh!" Judy giggled. "I'm still twenty-nine."

"Liar."

The nail techs asked them both to hold still for polish.

"He asked me out the other morning," Sofia said quietly. "After the whole kitten thing."

"What?" Judy squealed so loudly the manicurist nearly painted her ankle. "Sorry," she said. To Sofia she added, "And you said, 'Yes, please, now, oh god, take me?'"

"I said, 'No.'"

"So-feee-yah..." Judy drew out the syllables like she had when they were teens. "When a generally understood to be hot guy asks you out, you say, 'Yes.'"

Sofia gave her a withering glance.

Judy ignored her. "I'm serious. So what if you're only here for the season or whatever. He's gorgeous and funny and wants to go out with you. What could possibly be wrong with this scenario?" She swung her polished, separated, and flip-flopped feet over the side of the pedicure chair and waddled towards the drying benches. "And I have to know how he kisses. I bet he does things Christopher forgot about years ago."

"It wouldn't be a good idea, Jude. Really." Sofia followed suit.

"One of these days," Judy said solemnly, "you're going to have to stop running away from your father."

Judy saw past the carefully constructed version of herself she presented. Shame, guilt, and anger swirled up, and Sofia bit her tongue to keep from screaming at her childhood friend.

Instead, she tapped Judy's phone. "So, you have any pictures of your kids on there? I'm so bad about checking online."

———

JUDY'S LAST WARNING STAYED WITH HER FOR THE rest of the afternoon. When the July sun began to sink in the West, the Landing came alive. She sat behind the register, admiring her newly polished toenails between ringing sales and handing out colored golf balls. Behind her, she could hear her two teenage employees behind the snack bar. Gavin and Charlotte's flirtation was getting serious. They'd gotten to the giggle-and-bicker stage; it would only be a matter of time before she started stealing his baseball hat and he started trying to read her texts.

When Sofia had worked there, there hadn't been mobile phones, but she'd certainly stolen her fair share of baseball caps.

"What color did you pick?" Silas's voice pulled her out her speculative reverie.

He was in plaid shorts and a navy blue tee with "Maine" printed across his chest in academic lettering. She hadn't noticed his clothing earlier outside the nail salon. Of course, then he hadn't been standing under the flood lights, the sun-bleached streaks in his shoulder-length hair emphasized by the clear light, a day's stubble shadowing his jaw. Which she wasn't noticing now.

"Violet Crime," she replied. He had a hungry way of looking at her, like she was a pastry on a dessert cart. "Don't you have a business to run?"

"Theo's got the till for a minute, then I'm sending him out into the world. He's got tickets to some loud show at the Casino Ballroom tonight." He leaned over the counter. "And I did promise to come see you another time."

He smelled like laundry soap and cloves. She tried for cool. "Was that a promise or a threat?"

"Definitely a promise."

A group of golfers came through. Silas stayed casually to the side, making small talk with some of them.

Sofia was incredulous. "You really do flirt with everyone."

"It's just called manners," he said easily, "and being interested in people. It's good business."

"Is that it?" She asked dryly.

"Flirting aside, I'd like to buy you a drink, or dinner, or lunch; whatever's easiest."

"You aren't going to say, 'or breakfast?' and wink outrageously?" she countered snidely.

"I'd love to buy you breakfast," he said, raising an eyebrow, "but even for me, that's presumptuous. We haven't even had a first date."

"Are you always this arrogant?"

"Are you always this prickly?"

He'd gotten close. Dangerously close to the wall she'd only finished repairing after Judy's assault, temptingly close to her suddenly dry mouth and thudding pulse.

"Listen, Silas," she said. "I appreciate you being neighborly, and I'm glad you found your cat the other day, but I'm not interested in dating you."

She didn't expect the cocky smile. "Now who's being arrogant?"

"What?"

"I asked you out for a drink; you're already breaking up with me. Maybe I won't want to date you after we have drinks."

He was challenging her. She couldn't help taking the bait. It had been a long time since a man had gotten under her skin so quickly. "Trust me. If I wanted you to want to date me, you would."

Another group of prospective mini-golfers came through. Again, Silas chatted them up, finding out in the time it took to process a debit card where they were from, and how long they were staying.

When they'd left, he closed in on her again. "So what you're saying is, when we have drinks, if I come away wanting to date you, it's because you want me to?"

She smiled smugly. "That's exactly what I'm saying."

"Then you're saying yes to getting a drink with me." He looked positively triumphant. "I knew I'd talk you around."

"Wow." Sofia shook her head and frowned. "And no, that's not what I'm saying."

"When you frown like that, I want to kiss you."

He'd let his voice go husky, leaning across the counter. The breath left her lungs, and a delicious, anticipatory flutter raised gooseflesh on her arm.

"I've got to get back to the store. Theo's going to want to get going." He pushed away from the window. "Think about that drink, Sofia. I know I'm going to."

Three

Sofia woke to the crash and screech of the 5:00 a.m. garbage collection. By the time she parked her car in the High Hanover Garage in Portsmouth, she'd been up and busy for six hours. The quick walk from the garage to her real estate agent's storefront office gave her a few moments to soak in the near-forgotten ambiance of the seaside city.

"I'm reasonably confident we can sell quickly, especially with the property priced to move." Kevin Landry tapped a sheaf of paper on the desk, filed it in a binder, and slid it across his desk to her. "I've been selling commercial properties in this area for fifteen years, Ms. Buck. I've got a good sense of the market."

"I'm sure." She forced a smile, taking the listing contracts and stowing them in the briefcase tote she hadn't touched since she'd arrived in Hampton. The image of a briefcase in conjunction with the Landing gave her pause. There had been a developer with a briefcase once. He'd wanted to talk to her father about selling; Jimmy Buck had been sleeping off a case of Schlitz upstairs. Sofia had taken the man's brochure and promptly run him off.

"Mr. Landry, is there any way to guarantee the new owners won't make significant changes to the property?"

Kevin Landry templed his fingers. "That's a tricky question. They can't violate zoning, and I'm sure the property is grandfathered in to some old laws, but that's not to say with some wheel greasing it couldn't be torn down and rebuilt, or adapted into more of a condominium set up, even with the golf course."

She blew out a breath. Once it sold, it wasn't her problem.

He was watching her with concern. "I'm not sure why you're asking."

"I don't know. I was just curious." She trilled her fingertips on the desk, surprised not to hear the click of manicured nails. She'd been keeping them short and unpolished for a few weeks. The constant work of running the Landing wasn't kind to a manicure, and the only salon experience she'd had all summer was the recent pedicure with Judy. She stood, smoothing the hem of her top. "Thank you for your time, Mr. Landry. I look forward to closing this sale."

"Please, call me Kevin. Can I interest you in lunch?" He blushed, and Sofia really saw him for the first time that morning.

If Kevin Landry had been selling real estate for fifteen years, he must have started in his mid-twenties, she thought. He couldn't be more than forty. There was a sparkle in his blue eyes, hidden behind wire-rimmed glasses and a serious expression, and there was a hint of ropy strength in his tanned forearms, visible below the rolled up cuffs of his blue, Oxford dress shirt.

An excuse formed on her tongue. She was tired of fending off the men of southern New Hampshire. For a moment the night before, she'd honestly thought of giving in and taking Silas Wilde up on his obnoxious offer. At least Kevin Landry had asked her out like a gentleman. So, why not? How better to break the strange spell Silas had woven the night before?

"I'd like that."

Kevin blinked. His smile curved wide.

The diner next door to the real estate agent's office was new since Sofia's college days. It was decorated as if a three-year-old's imagination ran away with a '60s garage sale. It should been at odds with its boutique and gallery neighbors in the stately block of brick and stone offices, but it fit. The same way Colonial architecture rubbed up against the late nineteenth century, and the modern world slipped into the spaces between.

Over truly exceptional sandwiches, she answered his questions. "I'm an event planner for the DeVarona in D.C." She swirled a hand cut French fry in chunky homemade ketchup.

"But you grew up in the area?" Landry rattled the ice slightly in his iced coffee before he sipped.

"In the apartment on the third floor at Buck's Landing." She sniffed wryly, but a smile pushed at her cheeks.

"I love Hampton," he said. "I take my kids down on my weekends. We get fried dough at Blink's and they wear themselves out in the water."

She couldn't help looking at his left ring finger. He stretched out his naked hand.

"I've been divorced for five years. I've got a seven-year-old son and my daughter's eleven. My ex lives over the bridge in Kittery."

Sofia laughed at her own reaction. "I'm sorry. It's none of my business."

Kevin's smile turned tentative. "I wouldn't mind if it were."

Sofia sighed. He was a sweet man. "I'm flattered, Kevin. But I'm not staying. We're going to get Buck's Landing sold, and I'm going home to Washington."

"I understand." He delivered the reply with a professional smile.

The server came to take their empty plates. When dessert was offered, she declined.

"Thank you for lunch. I enjoyed myself, but I do need to get back to Hampton."

"It was my pleasure, Sofia." Kevin took the check from the server. "I'll take care of this. And I'll be in touch."

Sofia had a momentary flutter of guilt. Amy wasn't expecting her for another few hours. Outside, the sun was high, the sky azure and clear, the heat easy. A sudden craving for ice cream had her consulting her smartphone, not for the four dozen generic soft-serve flavors she sold at Buck's Landing, but real cream, hip-expanding ice cream piled into a sugar cone.

The contract in her bag weighed heavily on her as she walked. She'd surprised herself, with both the memory of the developer and the pang of guilt over the future of the Landing, followed by her refusal of Kevin Landry's kind and reasonably attractive offer for more than just a casual lunch. Her concern for the Landing's future, she could write off as mindful business practice, but it was Silas that kept her from saying yes to Kevin's quiet advance.

At the small ice cream parlor on Ceres Street, she ordered a double scoop of mint chocolate chip and decided to treat herself to a walking tour of Portsmouth on her way to the car. She hadn't been back to New Hampshire's port city in a decade, though it seemed little had changed except for a few newer businesses. As she walked, she considered Silas, trying to pinpoint how he'd gotten past her defenses.

She put him at just under six feet, with an athlete's body and a surfer's collar-length, shaggy blond waves. His blue-gray eyes were long-lashed, and his smile easy. More than the sum of his parts, though, she thought, pausing to look at a fuchsia dress in a shop window.

It was long, nearly floor-length on the mannequin, and the fabric looked soft and cool where it gathered at the empire waist. A summer vacation dress if ever she'd seen one. Taking a bite of her cone, she looked it over with a critical eye, but the dress invited fantasy. The skirt would flirt with her ankles, play peek-a-boo with her toes. The V-neck and high waistline would emphasize all her best curves. Slim satin straps would show off the rather impressive tan she'd gotten working her off-hours in a tank top all summer.

She tamped down the vision of an appreciative fire in Silas's eyes. Then she finished her ice cream and walked into the shop.

It was a summer for surprises, she told the cashier who rang up the sale. She hadn't come to Portsmouth to buy a dress. She hadn't come to New Hampshire to enjoy herself. She certainly hadn't come to Hampton to flirt with her next-door neighbor, but Silas hadn't gotten the memo. Ever since his troublesome cat had arrived at the Landing, he crept into her idle thoughts. His arrogant teasing, his determined flirting, ought to have set her teeth on edge, but she kept returning to how his gaze softened when he looked at her, to the humor in his eyes when he talked to his rebellious pet.

With her wallet lighter and her belly pleasantly heavier,

she found her car and headed for the interstate. At the first red light, she rolled down the BMW's windows and leaned her arm on the door, breathing in the salt and hot pavement scented air. Interstate 95 would bring her back to Hampton in half an hour, but the coastal road would only take fifteen minutes longer.

Halfway down Route 1-A, when the road swung up onto a rocky stretch of cliffs overlooking the sea in Rye, the memory of a forgotten night snuck up on her. The summer she was sixteen, she and Judy had driven up to Jenness State Beach, just for somewhere different to lie on the sand and wallow in Dave Matthews's voice.

Judy was already seventeen that summer, and had the keys to an '82 Volvo that maxed out at 45 miles an hour. It wasn't sexy, but it was a set of wheels. They'd loaded the trunk with Coke and Doritos, beach towels and baby oil. They'd camped out with a CD player boom box, a couple of old bedsheets, and no intention of getting in the water.

The boys who moved their Frisbee game over to get a better look were definitely older, and definitely prep-school boys.

When the disc landed near her feet, she looked up over her Cosmopolitan and did her best to seem worldly.

Behind his Oakleys, the emissary had playful chocolate eyes. "What are you two doing tonight?"

Someone's parents were away; someone else's brother was bringing kegs. The address was right on Ocean Boulevard, one of the mansions on the cliff.

They'd gone, walking to the address in their cutoffs and bikini tops, leaving Judy's station wagon in the state beach parking lot. They'd never found the boys from the beach, but they had found the beer and the shots of cheap vodka. Judy's older sister had come when they called her from a phone in the house. Hallie had sworn not to tell, but Sofia hadn't counted on her father.

She'd practically crawled up the stairs to the apartment and fallen through the door.

"Where the hell have you been?" Her father's eyes were closed, his head lolling on the back on the couch, but his voice was clear and his grip on the bottle was firm.

"A friend's house." She couldn't disguise the slur of alcohol and exhaustion.

"Bullshit, Sofia." He sucked in a ragged breath and she'd thought for one brilliant moment he was going to care that something might have happened to her. The desire for a good, old-fashioned grounding bloomed in her heart. He rolled his head and opened his eyes, narrowing his bleary gaze on her. "You have the early shift at the register tomorrow."

She'd pulled herself up and done her best to walk a straight line past her father's slumped form.

The memory carried her as far as the point where Ashworth Avenue split off from Ocean Boulevard, which was one-way going north along the boardwalk, but she drove the remaining blocks on autopilot. Swinging the car into the tiny parking lot she shared with her tenants, Sofia ducked into the snack bar to avoid passing the corner window of the Atlantis Market. It was time to get the Landing sold and behind her for good.

Silas wasn't waiting for her, but it was hard to miss the European purr of Sofia's car pulling into the narrow lot behind their buildings. When Sofia herself didn't appear on her steps, he tuned back in to his sister's monologue.

"I mean, I understand maybe you burned out at Stern & Lowe." This was a variation on the same speech she'd been giving him since he'd escaped New York after New Year's. "But Silas, you don't need to prove a point to anyone. Dad says Larry Holbein would take you on as a junior partner, or maybe you could work as a public defender if you want to save the world?" She straightened one of the slats on the cheap plastic Venetian blinds. "I'm sure you could sell this ... place, and come home. Theo says the store is doing well, I'm sure there's a market for it."

"Mal." Silas couldn't stop the warning from creeping into his tone.

"Or you could work on Senator Kingston's campaign." Her wheels were turning. "I could pull a few strings there."

"Mallory." He scooped Houdini up from his seat on the second hand coffee table. "Stop."

"Stop what? Trying to bring my baby brother to his senses?" She straightened the sofa cushion.

"I like it here. I hated New York. End of discussion."

She sat on the edge of the ratty sofa, crossing her legs and tapping her toe on the table. "What about when the money runs out?"

"It won't." He sat on the table opposite her, setting the gray cat down, and thanking the gods of Danish Modern furniture for their secondhand benevolence.

"How do you know?" Mallory leaned forward, searching for a chink in his armor.

"I'm going to be thirty this fall. I'm not your baby brother anymore." The bell jingled in the shop below. "Do you hear that? That was income, and that bell jingles all day long. The guy who sold me the place had everything in pristine shape, he was just old and tired. He cashed my check and moved to Myrtle Beach. All I have to do for now is keep doing what works."

"But what about after the summer?" She cast a woeful eye on the cheap replacement windows. "You aren't thinking about staying here all winter?"

"Not everyone wants a four bedroom Tudor on a Short Hills cul-de-sac, sis."

Mallory's expression shuttered. "What do you want?"

Houdini chose that moment to hop into Mallory's lap and start purring luxuriously. Silas thanked the little hairball for diffusing the situation. "I want to get a microchip for my escape artist cat. I want to breathe the air here for a while. I want to enjoy myself."

His sister ran a manicured hand down the kitten's spine. Houdini flexed his claws.

"I spent New Year's Eve prepping for a case." Silas got up and paced the small room. "I left the office at 1 a.m. I rode home in my Brooks Brothers suit and wool coat, on a train full of people celebrating. Kissing, drinking, fighting, laughing. Living, Mal. And I was working." He stopped and willed her to understand. "I bought the Jeep from a listing in the Want-Ads. I didn't even look at it first."

He waited for Mallory to interrupt. When she didn't, he went on.

"When I called you guys from Mystic, said I was taking some vacation time? I'd already found someone to sublet my apartment. A guy just like me. I hadn't traveled in five years. My fat salary? Sitting in well-researched investment accounts, where it very likely would have stayed until I met a nice girl and we got married and moved to Westchester."

Now Mallory's cheeks colored. "There's nothing wrong with that life."

He kept going, afraid she might derail him, even though she was finally listening. "The first time I skipped my every-six-weeks haircut? I took myself out for a beer down the road. I was wearing jeans and a sweater, my hair was a shade too long, and I was happy. Some guys invited me to play darts with them. They didn't even ask me my name. It was one of the best nights of my adult life."

"Silas." Mallory's tone softened.

"I stopped here because something about the icy beach called to me. I found this place by accident. But it feels right." He thought of Sofia. He could picture her all wrapped around him on the beach he loved. "And I think I met someone."

The smug married woman on his sofa snapped to attention. "Someone here?"

"Not exactly. She's from D.C." He fought the urge to look out his window toward the Landing. "But she's in town for a while."

"I can see you in Washington," Mallory said. Silas smiled. His sister was nothing if not determined.

"We'll see." He kept his voice light.

Mallory stood and wrapped him in a bear hug. She was twelve years older, and for his whole life she'd wanted to be a wife, a mother. She'd been married and rocking Theo to sleep in the starter home she and her husband had bought when Silas was just starting to sprout hair under his arms. Bossing him around was as natural to her as breathing. Silas wasn't even sure she knew she was doing it.

"I'm still leaving Theo here for the summer to keep an eye on you," she muttered into his shoulder.

"I love you." He squeezed her hard. "You're a nag, but I love you."

She smacked his chest. "My boy says he hasn't had a

decent meal in weeks. I'm taking you all out for dinner when the shop closes. Where?"

"We close at eleven tonight." Mallory's face fell, and he did some quick thinking. "Let me see if I can't find someone to cover the register for a couple of hours so I can join you."

"I bet we can get good lobster around here." Mallory tilted a lampshade true.

Silas chuckled. "The best. Let me walk you to your car."

He escorted his sister out through the store so she could embarrass Theo. After she kissed her son extravagantly, Silas hugged her, and walked with her across the street to the parking lot for the beach. He couldn't help sneaking a glance over his shoulder at Sofia's door. Like the frozen sand in January, something about her called to him, promising heat and pleasure if he stuck around long enough. Something about her felt right.

———

SOFIA WAS JUST ABOUT TO HEAD DOWN AND check on the snack bar and the register when she caught sight of Silas leaving the Market. He had his arm slung around a tall, athletic blonde. She wore her hair in an artfully messy ponytail, but Sofia knew a $200 cut-and-highlight when she saw one. The woman leaned into Silas's side, her face hidden for the moment. She had a deep, rich laugh; it drifted back on the sea breeze. Silas kissed the woman's forehead tenderly, and an ache lodged in Sofia's throat.

She pressed a hand to the glass as Silas walked his blonde companion around to the driver's side of a high-end SUV. The other woman ruffled Silas's hair. He closed the car door and patted the hood affectionately as she backed out. Sofia reminded herself of her earlier promise. Her neighbor was undeniably under her skin, but that was no reason to delay her plans to unload the property and return to her hard-won life-in-progress. She didn't belong in Hampton now anymore than she had when she left.

She arrived in the snack bar to Silas's easy banter. He was trading a five for a large twist cone. Charlotte was working the ice cream window, and Gavin, whose day off it was, was loitering around. From just outside the staff entrance, Sofia held her silence watching Gavin preen, trying to distract Charlotte, who clearly liked being the focus of Silas's attention.

"Gavin, you interested in a few hours work?" Silas asked.

The boy squared his shoulders. "Sure. What kind?"

Silas caught a drip of his soft-serve. "I need someone to cover the till at the Atlantis while I let a beautiful woman take me to dinner." He winked broadly. "Since Charlotte here is working and can't be my date."

Charlotte flushed pink. She was newly seventeen, just barely old enough to work the evening shift. Her budding romance with Gavin, also seventeen, was the stuff of teen magazine dreams. Gavin was from nearby Salisbury, Massachusetts, which despite being two towns away, might as well be another planet when school started in the fall. Sofia felt strangely protective of them. Her own teenage years had been balanced so precariously between those youthful infatuations and the immense heartbreak that was her family.

Gavin was nodding at Silas. "I can do that. When do you need me?"

Sofia loitered in the hallway, watching Charlotte watch the men make their arrangements. Silas's cheerful banter with the teens charmed her, even while she hated the gorgeous blonde in the Lexus who was his actual date. He tipped his sunglasses at Charlotte before taking his leave. Gavin was fast on his heels, but he turned quickly.

"Charlotte? I'll stop by to get you when I'm done."

The young woman beamed. "I'll be here."

When the men were gone, Sofia went over the day's sales with Charlotte. The snack bar did a brisk business in cones and sundaes, even with non-mini-golf customers.

Charlotte was a chatty girl, and Sofia had learned to filter out much of the gossipy prattle, but Silas's name caught her attention as she was filing through the receipts.

"I think it's really sweet that he likes to hang out with his sister."

Sofia frowned. "What?"

"Oh, Silas, Mr. Wilde, was in here just before you got here. He hired Gavin to watch the store for a while so he and Theo—isn't Theo cute? So they could go out to dinner with his sister Mallory. Theo's from New Jersey. I think Gavin might be a little jealous of him, since he's in college, and he's all ripped from playing soccer."

Sofia laughed, interrupting Charlotte's monologue. "How do you know all this stuff?"

"I pay attention."

Sofia grinned. "You certainly do. Keep that up, it's a good life skill."

Silas's sister Mallory from New Jersey. She flushed slightly at her own jealousy.

Satisfied that Charlotte was handling the ice cream window fine on her own, she went to relieve Amy at the golf-course register. The dinner hours were sometimes slow, so she settled into her seat, picking up the novel Amy had been reading in her down time. It was about twenty years old, with a tall, dark, chiseled hero on the cover, and the title in gilded lettering. At the end of two hours, she was a good way through it.

"I wouldn't have pegged you for a reader of bodice-rippers." Silas was leaning on the chain link gate that separated the course from the sidewalk on that side. She was unreasonably glad to see him.

"I thought you had a date." She hoped her reply sounded flip.

His eyes twinkled. "I did. Steamers and lobster down at the pound with my sister and my nephew." He waved through to Charlotte, who'd seen him from her position at the snack bar window.

Sofia set the book down, bending its broken spine. "Do you flirt with everyone on the strip?"

Silas laughed, crossing to the cashier's window and leaning in. "Just the pretty girls."

"I'm sure." She sat up a little straighter. "Are you going to make a habit of hanging out at my gate?"

"Maybe. I have another date tomorrow night," he said with a sly grin.

"Oh?" She didn't want to hear about it.

"I'm taking her to Blink's for fried dough, and then I'm going to kick her ass at Skeeball down at the Funarama," he said, dropping his voice to a conspiratorial whisper. "But just so she doesn't get mad at me, I'm going to win her a giant stuffed panda at the ring toss."

"You seem awfully sure of yourself," she countered.

"Oh, I am." He straightened, but reached out to push a stray lock of hair, gone curly in the humidity, from her cheek. "I'll pick you up at ten-fifteen, after the course closes."

He was gone before she even had a chance to reply.

Four

Silas was punctual. He knocked on her door at quarter after ten. The night was balmy, the heat soft like velvet. Sofia spent several minutes after her rinse-off in the shower stall debating whether to wear the fuchsia dress, but the threat of greasy boardwalk treats won the night.

He greeted her with a stem of gladiolus. "Hi."

She took the flowers, lips bending up even as she fought appearing delighted. "Thank you. I'm just about ready."

The stem was too big for any of her mother's vases, but there was an iced tea pitcher on top of the fridge that would hold it.

Silas waited for her in the doorway, backlit by the glow of the boardwalk below. Sofia gave the flowers some water and turned to him. "Shall we?"

Ocean Boulevard was never quiet in the summer. They stepped out onto the street and were swept into the current. A pod of teenagers in band tee shirts drifted ahead of them, mugging for photos that would end up online in a heartbeat. A family passed them, the sunburnt father carrying a sleeping child while the mother pushed a baby in a stroller that looked like a spaceship. Silas reached for her hand at the fourth cross-street.

"I thought there was Blink's Fry Doe on the agenda?" Sofia asked impishly, looking at their joined hands.

"Later," Silas promised, leading her towards a loud neon sign. "First, a drink."

The Salty Cod was as dark inside as the sign outside was bright. It was full, but not crowded. A four-piece cover band was crammed into one corner, a beautiful woman on lead vocals covering Bonnie Raitt. The ache in her delivery made Sofia wish she could sing. Silas waved at the bartender as they approached, then leaned in close. "What do you want?"

Sofia stretched up on her toes to look at the drafts. "Blue Moon."

Up close, the bartender looked familiar. He caught her eye as he took their drink orders. "Sofia?"

She squinted a little as the past crept up on her again. "Decker?"

The bartender's laugh nearly drowned out the band. "Sofia Buck back on the strip and in my bar! What are you doing back in town?"

"I..." Her glib response dried up on her tongue. Her father was dead and she was here to sell his legacy, possibly to some developer who would tear down her Grandfather's piece of this scrap of coastline.

Decker saw the pause. "Hey, I heard about your Dad. I'm really sorry."

"Thanks, Dex," she said softly.

"So you two know each other?" Silas asked.

Sofia laughed. "Sorry. Silas Wilde, Dex Adams."

Decker slid their glasses across the bar on cardboard coasters. "I know this clown. He hustled his way into a darts game a few months ago and we haven't been able to shake him yet."

"How you doing tonight?" Silas exchanged a twenty for the beers.

"Pretty good." Decker mopped the wet streaks on the bar. "Can't complain."

"So," Silas asked, "How do you guys know each other?"

Decker answered first. "Sofi here taught me how to kiss." He waggled his eyebrows at her from under a worn Bruins cap. "Back when we were too young to know anything about anything."

"Really?" Silas grinned. "Tell me more."

"She busted my ass about having no finesse." Decker poured a few drinks for other patrons. "Worked, too. Married a farmer's daughter I met up at UVM. She's a pediatrician now, and our little guy is three and a half."

"That's great, Dex." Sofia had forgotten the couple of months in high school when she and Decker couldn't keep their hands, or their mouths, off one another.

"In fact, seeing as you crafted me into the fine specimen of manhood I am today, the next round's on me."

Sofia blushed.

"It's good to have you back in town, Sof." Decker nodded at Silas. "Now, go teach this joker a thing or two, okay?"

"I think I'm jealous," Silas whispered in her ear, "but it seems I have Dex's blessing."

Her flush deepened. "That's not what that was," she hissed.

"That's exactly what it was." Silas sipped the foam off his Sam Adams. "Can I get a lesson tonight?"

He was trying to get a rise out of her; she smirked. "If you win me that giant panda, you're on."

"I love a challenge." Silas raised his glass. She clinked hers against it.

They left the bar after the second round, while the band was breaking. Someone was lighting Roman candles on the beach and Sofia watched the fireworks reflect over the small whitecaps at the edge of the water.

"You love this place, don't you?" Silas's question was gentle, but the punch of guilt and fear that rushed through was anything but.

"I loved this place," she corrected, turning away from the pyrotechnics and moving forward. "Past tense. I had some good times, but that was a long time ago."

She slowed on the corner of H Street, giving the orange awning at Blink's a meaningful look, but Silas kept walking.

"Not yet. Fry Doe slows my reaction time down." His lips grazed her ear, sending a shiver down her spine. "And I have a panda to win."

Sofia's thoughts dried up en route from her brain to her lips. Instead, she let anticipation coast down her body, settling low in her belly.

The noise and the heat inside the Funarama were overwhelming after the cooler humidity of the boardwalk. Silas fed twenty dollars to a change machine like a professional. He scooped the quarters into his pocket. "You pick the machines, so we both know I didn't cheat when I kick your butt." He counted out half the quarters and handed them over to her.

Sofia picked the slightly older Skeeball machines at the end of the line. The smell of the raw plank floors drifted up as she dropped a quarter into her machine and pressed start. The balls clinked into place; the marquee lit up. Silas did the same. His smile was wolfish.

For the first few tosses, she lagged behind. She was more

than ten years out of practice. True to his word, Silas was racking up forty- and fifty-point throws, tickets rolling out of his machine at a gleeful rate. She glared at his celebratory dance when his first two games bested her by well over five hundred points.

GOD, SHE'S GORGEOUS, SILAS THOUGHT, watching her brow furrowed in concentration. He'd been paying attention and her scores were quietly improving. He'd have to step up his game; his pride was on the line. She bent to feed the machine, the long tail of her French braid trailing over her shoulder.

Her camisole hugged her breasts, teased the top of her hip-hugging denim capris. His sister would call those shoes slingbacks, or maybe wedges; Silas just appreciated the lean line of muscle and golden skin from ankle to knee. Her toenails were still painted shocking purple, and she wore a slightly tarnished ring around her pinky toe. Somehow, that dulling silver stoked the fire glowing hot and steady in his gut. She banked her first ball and squealed as it dropped cleanly into the coveted one-hundred point spot.

Sofia gave him an I-dare-you smile and picked up her second ball. Just as she tossed, he leaned over to kiss the spot behind her ear. The ball went wild, clattering into the ten-point hole.

"Cheater!" Indignity suited her. He wondered if the spots of color on her cheeks were embarrassment or arousal.

"All's fair in war and Skeeball." He dropped another quarter into his machine, focusing on the forty.

More than a few rounds later, Silas dropped his last quarter in. "Last round. Can you take another beating?"

Sofia tore off her strip of tickets. "Uncle. You win. For now."

"For now?" The devilish twinkle in her eyes intrigued him. The digital calliope beckoned and he tossed three fifties in a row. Winding up for a fourth, he felt Sofia press up against him on his left side.

"I'm not that easily distracted," he assured her.

"If you say so." She bit his shoulder on the toss and the ball jumped two machines, rolling haplessly across the floor before coming to rest under Ms. Pac Man.

He circled her waist with one arm and hauled her close. "You fight dirty." He'd only meant a quick contact, a little reminder of the simmering attraction between them, but Sofia held him there. She opened her lips against his, something between a moan and a purr rumbling in her throat, before rocking back on her heels. A Funarama employee was holding out Silas's lost ball.

The boy's eyes took an adolescent tour of Sofia's curves. Silas took the ball with a sharp look, contemplating pinging it off the pimply kid's skull.

Sofia missed the exchange. She was fiddling with her bundle of Skeeball tickets. "Are we turning them in now?" she asked, "Or can we play something else?"

"What's your game?" She was surveying the game floor with the seriousness of an art collector in a gallery. There was a faint sheen of sweat at her hairline, and a stray hair that had fallen from her braid curled against her neck. Silas resisted the urge to tug the black band from her hair and let all those glossy dark brown curls tumble over her shoulders.

She chose the Wheel.

"I'm feeling lucky." She fished in her pocket. "One last quarter. Think I can hit the jackpot?"

"Nope." He loved watching the fight rise in her eyes, loved watching humor temper it.

"If I get it, I get all your Skeeball tickets, too. How's that for a bet?"

"You're on," he said. "But if you miss, I get all of yours."

"Done."

When she dropped her coin into the machine and sent the light spinning along its path, Silas felt something slip into place in his heart. He wouldn't have found her in New York, slaving away to the paper gods of justice. He wouldn't have found her in the overpriced clubs or the dive bars his buddies favored. He wouldn't have found her at his father's country club in New Jersey.

She was here. And she didn't even realize it.

"Holy shit!" Sofia jumped up and squeezed him, her giddy laughter in his ear. "I won!"

He held her there, painted toes off the floor, drinking in the spicy, elemental fragrance of her warm hair. Her body pressed against his, and he could feel unbridled pleasure at the win flying along her skin, pulsing through her. He couldn't imagine there being anything better than this. Everything about her just fit.

The Wheel was spitting out a seemingly endless reel of tickets. All the adults, and a few of the kids, around them stopped to see what the commotion was. Reluctantly, Silas set her down. Raising her hand like a triumphant prize fighter, he addressed the small crowd.

"She won the Wheel."

Sofia tore off her tickets and held out her hand. With a little bow, he handed her the stack of folded tickets from his pocket. She took them and turned for the prize counter, but not before taking his hand to tow him behind her.

They didn't have enough for a panda, but Sofia traded her tickets in for a perfectly horrible purple glass mermaid statue. When Silas laughed, she very seriously informed him that the mermaid was for the cashier's window at the Landing.

"Well, in that case, she's perfect."

Sofia tucked the mermaid into her straw purse. "To the ring toss?"

"How about the milk bottles? I'm feeling like a sure thing."

Sofia's wry smile was worth the bad joke.

The hawker was a guy in his early twenties. These days the hawkers worked the crowd with a headset, but the essential game was unchanged. Silas handed him a five for three chances. He felt like a high school kid again, trying to impress a beautiful girl with his athletic prowess. Sofia leaned against the counter, watching him gauge the throw. In the bright lights of the midway, she could have been a high school girl, too.

His first ball went a little to the left, but it nicked a bottle hard enough to knock over the first pyramid. He squared his shoulders.

When the third pyramid of bottles clattered to the floor of the booth, Silas whooped. He whirled Sofia off her feet, giving her a smacking kiss before setting her down again.

"So," asked the hawker, "what would the lady like?" He gestured to the row of super-sized animals hanging above.

"The panda." They spoke together, giggling as the hawker fetched it down. Sofia hugged it hard, and Silas was reminded of the deal they'd made in Dex's bar.

"You two have a good night." The hawker sent them off, already drawing in new players for the game.

Silas struck out for H Street. "Come on, panda girl. Let's get you some fried dough."

Sofia couldn't remember being so happy in Hampton, not since she was a child. With the panda looped under her arm, she walked in easy time with Silas. At the first cross street, he reached for her hand.

Blinks was a blaze orange shrine to fried dough. The porch overhang was crowded with people waiting for orders; the line stretched down the stairs into the sidewalk.

"What do you want?" Silas asked.

She handed him the stuffed panda. "This is on me."

Silas took the bear. "Cinnamon and sugar."

She snuck a glance at him while he leaned against the signpost. As if he felt her eyes on him, he turned to her. The street light threw his face into deep shadows, but his intent was unmistakable. She shivered, understanding pooling low in her belly.

Rejoining him with the fried dough, she gestured across the street, where several empty benches lined the beach boardwalk. Silas set the panda down to one side to take his fried dough. He looked at hers, brows raised. "Cinnamon sugar and powdered sugar?"

She nodded. "The only way to have it." The first bite was perfect, crisp from the fryer, soft inside, sugary and sweet. She hummed with pleasure.

"Remind me to take you for fried dough more often," Silas said, sinking his teeth into his own.

They ate in silence, watching the amateur fireworks displays from the beach, followed by the Hampton police on their quads breaking up the lawbreakers. She started to hand Silas a napkin, but he licked the sugar and cinnamon from his fingers with a wink. Sofia swore she could feel his mouth on her own skin.

"Look," Silas said pointing to the sky above them.

A red Chinese lantern drifted over the beach. It caught a column of air and spiraled gently up before flying out over the Atlantic. They watched it until it burned out over the horizon.

"I've never seen one before," Sofia whispered. "Not like that."

"Me neither." Silas stood, snagging the panda by one plush paw. "Come on. Let's walk home on the beach, see if we can find where they're launching them.

They walked along the boardwalk until they reached a set of stairs down to the sand. Without speaking, they stopped to take their shoes off. Bare-footed, they set out southward on the beach.

"They grant wishes," she said. "Or they can."

As they walked, a new pair of lanterns rose from the far side of the dunes at the southernmost end of the state park parking lot.

"What's your wish?" Silas asked.

To have my parents back. The thought surfaced quickly, taking her by surprise. Unwanted tears pricked the bridge of her nose. She took a deep breath. It felt wrong, under a sky full of stars and paper wishes, to lie. "I wish I'd had the chance to say goodbye to my dad."

Yet again, Silas took her hand in his. He squeezed gently, offering silent comfort.

"I'd try to forgive him." The confession made her light-headed. "I wish I could have told him that I missed her, too, but that I needed him, and I was so angry, so sad, and so alone. So goddamn jealous of the booze."

Silas stopped, dropped the panda, and smoothed his warm hands over her shoulders. His face swam in and out of focus through her tears.

"He knew, Sofia."

She blinked, letting the tears take their course.

"He knew," Silas said again. "He might not have spoken about it, but I'm sure he knew. He was sober, Sofia, and he worked his tail off. He filled that apartment with photographs. He wore his memories like a hair shirt."

"Why?" Her voice caught. "Why are you telling me this?"

"Because it's eating you up." He pulled her close, lips brushing her temple. "Forgive him. Let him go."

"I wish I could." She stepped out of the embrace. "I hope I can."

Silas's whispered kiss at her temple burned like a brand. There was nowhere to look but his face, nothing to do with her hands, and then he reached for her, brushing her knuckles with his thumb. He dropped his shoes on the sand and traced her jaw with his finger.

His lips were cool, his tongue sweet from the fried dough. His hands slipped under the hem of her top, skimming the small of her back. He slipped his fingers through the straps of her slingbacks, unwinding her grip and dropping them near his sandals. She tipped her head, wrapped her arms around his neck and drew the kiss in deeper. The gentle simmer of desire between them boiled over, seasoned with a little desperation. Tonight, she wanted him. Consequences be damned.

He breathed in the touch of perfume she wore at her clavicle. "Totally worth a panda."

He reached down, cupping her ass and pulling her up against him. She smiled against his mouth; he wanted her just as badly. Her lashes fluttered when his teeth nipped at her lower lip. Overhead, the lanterns soared. She braced her hands on his forearms.

"Silas."

His response was low and hoarse. "Yeah."

She scooped up her shoes and walked down to the water's edge. When Silas's expression asked her an unspoken why, she laughed. "I can walk faster on the wet sand."

Mischief. She saw it in his eyes, and then he rushed her, reaching down for his sandals and the bear as he did. He slung her over one shoulder and ran down the tide line. She shrieked, giddy laughter bubbling up along with the salt spray from his feet in the waves. After a hundred feet, he set her down, panting and grinning.

Sofia pushed a few stray strands of hair off her face. "That's one way to get home faster."

Silas regained his breath. "Not fast enough." He kissed her purposefully.

Behind him, a campfire flickered in its copper fire pit. Sofia knew the spot from her evening walks on the beach. A group was lighting and releasing the Chinese lanterns behind one of the rental cottages on Haverhill. This time, she took his hand. "What's your wish?"

Silas looked meaningfully at Buck's Landing's sign beckoning from down the beach, and ran with her toward them. "We're almost there."

They tumbled through her door, blood hot and pulses racing. Her bag and the panda fell forgotten just inside the apartment. Sofia pushed his faded Princeton tee up, baring his chest. She ran her nails through the soft hair there. Their arms tangled in their hasty efforts to get to skin. His teeth scraped her jaw, nipped at her neck and shoulders.

Sofia shivered when he pulled her tank top over her head, heat like mercury pooled between her thighs and she tugged at the button of his khaki shorts. Silas stepped out of them even as he was pushing denim down over her hips. Breathless, they paused; he in his cotton boxers, she in a few scraps of lace.

Slowly, so slowly, he reached up and behind her neck. He tugged the elastic from her braid, twisting it between his fingers briefly before tossing it on the nearby coffee table. When he reached for her again, she stilled his hands. Without a word, she threaded her fingers into the braid and shook it free, her curls tumbling down over her shoulders with a little toss of her head.

He came into her arms and she pressed them both down into the faded leather sofa. Straddling his lap, she reached back to undo her bra. He filled his hands with her breasts, thumbs grazing the soft well of flesh. From beneath lashes grown heavy with lust, she watched him take one aching nipple into his mouth. With the first touch of wet heat and the scrape of his teeth, she was ready for him. She reached between them, caressing him through his boxers.

Silas left her breast to lay a trail of damp kisses along her collarbone, to tease her lips, to torture her with sweetness. Her blood sang; her skin was on fire. His hands, which slipped under what satin remained, found her slick and wanting; everything about his onslaught left her breathless.

He kissed from her lips to her ear, whispering low. "Do you have anything?"

She sat up on her knees. "This way."

Her feet had barely touched the floor when a shrill yowl split the night. Silas sat up. "What the hell?"

He slipped back into his shorts and out onto her landing; wrapping a blanket around herself, she stepped out behind him. A thrashing bundle of fur and claws was scrapping in the narrow concrete lane between Buck's Landing and the Atlantis Market.

"Shit." Silas stuffed his feet into his sandals. "Houdini!"

His feet thumping on the stairs broke up the spat between his tiny ball of fury and a skinny marmalade that streaked away down the block. Sofia watched him coax Houdini out of the shadows. Even from her vantage point, she could see the ridge of raised fur along the kitten's spine.

Silas looked up at her with a pained expression. "I'll make it up to you."

"Not if I make it up to you first," she said. She tried for flirtatious, but disappointment pressed against her ribcage. She loitered in her own doorway as Silas unlocked his back door and disappeared inside with the angry cat.

Picking up her scattered clothes a few moments later, she realized Silas had left his shirt. With a foolish smile, she inhaled his scent from the fabric. She left the Princeton tee folded on her sofa, but the fragrance of sunshine, sand, and soap stayed with her until she fell asleep.

Five

Sofia was sweeping the sidewalk under the awning when the tenants from 2A, a French-Canadian couple down from Montreal for the week, passed by, headed out for a morning whale watching trip.

"Bonjour, Sofie," waved Catherine, trailing her husband towards their sporty green car. "We'll bring you a whale!"

The charming Gallic elegance in the Gaultier's English put visions of wine, Brie, baguettes, and perfect bites of dark, silky chocolate into Sofia's head. For all she knew, Catherine Gaultier had just such a picnic stashed away in her sailor-striped canvas tote.

The set up at the Landing allowed for both the Snack Bar and the Mini-Golf to operate out of the food-service window when she was understaffed. Since she was on her own until her teenaged employees arrived, Sofia set out the sign redirecting golf traffic to the Snack Bar. She busied herself setting up the soft-serve machines, industrial coffeemaker, and beverage cooler before opening the register.

It occurred to her, not for the first time, that it wasn't so much a snack bar as an ice cream window, but her dad hadn't been much for marketing specifics. She was three lines into a list of fresh names when her first customers arrived, and she remembered that the Landing's future wasn't up to her.

She handed the family their scorecard and brightly colored golf balls and directed them around the building to the first tee. "Enjoy your game," she called.

"This morning looks good on you."

She turned to Silas, who'd come up to the counter. There was a blush in her voice when she replied. "Good morning. How's Houdini?"

"No worse for wear, but patrolling the egresses for any sign of his arch nemesis. I'm going to have to bar the windows."

Sofia had to laugh.

"I only have a minute," he said, reaching into his pocket and pulling out a newspaper wrapped package and setting it on the counter, "but I thought this guy might be a friend for your mermaid."

She unfolded the newspaper to reveal a goofy clay statue of a lobster wearing swim trunks and carrying a pail and shovel. She was laughing when she thanked Silas. "He'll look great over on my desk."

Silas leaned over the counter and peered at the military surplus desk that served as operations center for Buck's Landing. The purple glass mermaid already sat admiring her sandblast-textured tail under the desk lamp. "I see she's already made herself at home."

Sofia got up to settle in her new crustacean friend. She couldn't think when Silas got close like that, not with the memory of what had nearly happened between them thick around her like fog. "He'll be good company for her."

"Maybe she'll like it so much, she'll decide to stay."

Sofia raised an eyebrow. "Maybe she wants to see the world."

"You know what I want?" Silas didn't move, but she felt the floor shift under her at his intimate tone. Her thoughts scattered.

"Do I want to know?" Even to her ears, it was a lame reply.

"Yeah. You do." His expression scorched what remained of her scattered thoughts. "Besides that, I'd like to have dinner together. Is there a night you can slip away?"

Sofia glanced at the color-blocked wall calendar over her desk. "Amy's got the Thursday evening shift and both kids are coming in."

"Thursday, then," Silas said. "You want me to make reservations?"

The idea sprang, fully formed, into her head. "No. I'll cook. My place at eight."

If Silas was surprised, he was smart enough not to show it.

———

AMY'S THURSDAY SHIFT STARTED AT THREE, AND Sofia was bound for Exeter by a quarter after. She dialed Judy's number on a whim.

"What's up?" Judy sounded drowsy.

"Oh no, I woke you!" Sofia said. "I'm so sorry."

"Don't worry about it, really, I'd much rather talk to you."

Sofia soaked in Judy's affection. "I'm going over to

61

Exeter to the farmer's market. What's your afternoon look like?"

"The boys are coming home from camp with my mom, and the baby's napping." She paused, when she spoke again, the sleep was gone from her voice. "Are you inviting me?"

Sofia laughed, which Judy correctly interpreted as a yes. "Give me two minutes."

She disconnected the call, but when Sofia checked Judy's text at the next red light, she got her answer.

Mom staying. I'll be waiting

And waiting she was, in shorts, sneakers, and a tank-top, with a huge market basket looped over her arm, leaning against a gray VW at the end of the driveway. Sofia realized with a start that the license plate was the same one that had been on the old Volvo Judy had driven in high school. She never had a chance to ask after Judy's parents. Judy hopped into the Beamer before Sofia had time to put it in neutral.

"You weren't kidding!"

"About waiting?" Judy snorted. "Hell no. I never joke about being freed from the yoke of my maternal duties."

They drove for a few minutes in relative quiet, enjoying the radio and the cloudless day.

It had been a long time, but Judy still knew her so well. "So, what's the occasion?"

"I decided I wanted to cook. You remember how good my mom's marinara was? She grew her tomatoes, though." Sofia never took her eyes from the road. "I didn't have time to grow tomatoes this summer, but if I'm going to buy them, I wanted to get as close to that as I could."

Judy wasn't buying her casual tone. "You just decided it

was time to revive your mother's marinara recipe? On a random Thursday in late July?"

"So what if I did?" Sofia replied with what she hoped was indifference.

"Bullshit." Judy shifted in the passenger seat to face her. "Did you finally give in to that hunky neighbor of yours?"

"Give in?"

"You said you turned him down last time, and it's been a while. I figure," she clapped her hands together, "he's the determined type."

Sofia realized that Judy already knew. "And Dex told you he saw us the other night in the bar."

Judy took a breath. "And Dex told me he saw you two the other night at the bar." She frowned. "I can't believe you weren't going to tell me."

Sofia sighed. "I kind of suck at confiding. I'm out of practice."

"Don't you worry," Judy said, squeezing her hand, "I'll get you back into shape."

The farmer's market was packed with shoppers. Sofia was as tempted by Swasey Park's view of the Squamscott River as she was by the local offerings. Sofia and Judy walked the row of tents, carts and vans, spilling over with produce at the height of the summer growing season. Though the tomatoes were just beginning to peak, she found the requisite poundage of firm, dimpled, scarlet fruit.

They filled Judy's basket with the tomatoes, onions, basil, and fresh bread. Judy introduced her to a woman who made soaps, and a collective of local crafters who brought quilted, knit, and crocheted items to the market. To Sofia's delight, there was even a handmade pasta vendor. She bought a pound of tagliatelle to go with the sauce.

Judy was a keen observer.

"You know, if it's true what they say about men's hearts and their stomachs, I'd say you were trying to seduce to the poor creature."

Sofia treated them to fresh coffee and sugared donuts still warm in brown paper bags. They ate sitting on the hood of the BMW in the sunshine.

"I'm glad you called," Judy said, licking sugar from her fingers.

"I'm glad I called, too." Sofia rolled up the paper bag and lobbed it at a nearby trash can. It bounced in off the rim.

"And you'll call me and tell me how it goes?"

"Are we sixteen?" Sofia arched a brow.

Judy giggled. "If that's what it takes. That man is scrumptious."

"You clearly need to get laid."

Judy laughed out loud at Sofia's tart reply. "Christopher does okay in that department. Don't fear for me. I just like to indulge in a little secondhand single-girl sex." She got up to throw away her own trash. "You know, the kind that doesn't require a bolted door or a babysitter."

Underneath her friend's grumbling, Sofia heard the deep satisfaction of someone who had exactly what she wanted. The realization was bittersweet. Maybe in a different lifetime, she could have been happy like that, too.

Sofia's mother's recipe box was still on the shelf over the three-quarter size refrigerator from the late '70s that still dominated the apartment kitchen. The cards inside were still floury, her mother's touch preserved in the pale, dusty film. The tomatoes glistened in the colander in the sink. The big stockpot sat, washed and dried, on the range. She'd sharpened her mother's favorite knives. All that remained was to cook.

She began to read the card marked "Nonna's Marinara." Her mother's gentle, elegant script drew her back through the years. As a child, with every passing year, she'd been able to help with some new step in the process. The last summer before her mother died, she'd been allowed to dice the onions and supervise the blanching of the tomatoes. Now, as she worked, her body and her memory recreated the steps, filling in the secrets her mother had never written down on the cards.

Though a few tears seasoned it, Sofia was content when the sauce was simmering quietly a few hours later. She tidied up a little, and then put up another big pot for pasta. Salty like the sea, her mother had told her, pouring a long silver-white waterfall of salt into the cooking water.

She put the bread, wrapped in foil, into the oven and opened a bottle of Valpolicella she'd brought from Washington. All she needed now was music. She was halfway to her purse for her iPod when she remembered her mother bending to touch the needle to the scratchy vinyl LPs she'd loved so much. Leaving the wine to breathe on the counter, Sofia ventured into her parents' room to look for them.

The boxes with the old records were in her father's closet. Sofia was digging through the LPs when there was a knock on the door.

Silas stood on her landing in the hibiscus-print shorts she'd first seen him in, this time paired with a faded country club tournament tee shirt. He carried a bakery box and a sunflower under his arm.

"I could smell dinner from the sidewalk." He leaned in

to kiss her cheek. "I might be the luckiest guy on the strip tonight."

"You just might be," she said. "But you have to earn your keep."

He snaked an arm around her waist and pulled her close, whispering against her mouth. "I can do that."

She felt the scarlet blush rise up her face. "No, not that. I opened a box of records in my parents' room. Go pick out some music."

He left her with his offerings and disappeared into the other room.

Sofia trimmed the sunflower's stem and set it into one of the milk glass vases still decorating the bookshelf. The longer she stayed in the apartment, the more she saw that her father had made it his own, but carefully kept bits of his wife's memory alive. Little touches, like her recipe box and her knickknacks, still adorned the shelves. Framed photographs were everywhere in a riot of faded snapshots from her early childhood and glossy 4"x6" prints from the years closer to her mother's passing.

Silas came in bearing an armful of records.

"I can see what he loved about her," he said. "I mean, your mother was a knockout, and she loved Dusty Springfield."

Sofia grinned. "She had a killer marinara recipe, too."

"Where's the record player?" Silas cast around for evidence of stereo equipment.

"Right there." Sofia pointed behind him to an antique console player that occupied one wall of the living room. Silas went a little pink around the ears.

"No Dusty?" Sofia asked when the Lovin' Spoonful filled the room.

"She's for later," he said, wrapping his arm around her

and resting his chin on her shoulder while she stirred the sauce. Sofia couldn't help but shiver.

She turned in his embrace and laid her palms on his cheeks. "Now? Make yourself useful and set the table."

I COULD GET USED TO THIS, SILAS THOUGHT, scooping up the last of Sofia's sauce with a heel of bread. Her lashes brushed her cheeks when she tipped her wineglass to swallow the last of the bright, cranberry-colored wine. He got up to switch the record, finding an old Simon & Garfunkel album that reminded him of the wood-paneled rec room in his parents' first house in New Jersey. His sister had loved all the old records their parents kept down there, playing everything from psychedelic rock to disco when he was too young to really care.

"We may have to save the lemon bars for another time," he said, patting his stomach. "That was a great dinner."

"Lemon bars?" Sofia's lips curved up, and he resolved to bring her baked goods more often.

They cleared the table together. Sofia loaded the dishwasher as Silas gathered up the table settings. He untied the strings from the bakery box and the sugary tang of the lemon bars wafted out. Sofia was scrubbing out the sauce pot when Silas slipped out of the kitchen.

"I know what will go perfectly with those," she called.

"Me too," he replied, coming back in. He pulled her hands out of the soapy water and wrapped them in a dishtowel. "Dance with me."

He led her to the console and dropped the needle. Dusty Springfield's soulful croon soared out over horns and close backup harmonies. Silas drew Sofia close. He led her effortlessly, silently thanking the dance classes he'd taken for PE credit in college.

They turned and swayed, their bodies in tune for three aching minutes while Dusty begged her lover to "just be close at hand." Silas could feel the blood move under her skin, smell her perfume and shampoo. Her soft cotton top shifted against his hand on the small of her back. When she laid her cheek against his chest, the warmth of her breath set his pulse jumping. The track ended, but, instead of releasing her, he ended the dance with a searching kiss.

Need rose up around them like fog, blinding them to all but each other. Her touch honey-slow, ghosting over his body, their breath mingling, the flavor of desire flooding his senses. All this while they undressed one another, drawing out the anticipation. Yearning for her rushed through him.

Silas wasn't sure how they had gotten there when his calves bumped her mattress. Seeking more than the dance, he caught her up and rolled them both across the bed. Sofia laughed between kisses, but her laughter faded into a deep shudder when he slid her underwear off. Shucking his own, he joined her, wrapping her in his arms. "Remind me to give Houdini an extra catnip mouse for introducing us."

"At least he didn't interrupt tonight," Sofia said.

"I'd have left his bony ass on the welcome mat this time," Silas growled.

"Yeah, right." Sofia giggled again, and then he was touching her. Laughter went up in a flame of sheer pleasure when he filled her. She drew him into the fire until they were both spent.

He dozed afterward, with Sofia warm and sleepy at his side, waking to an unexpected rumble in his belly.

Her whisper told him she wasn't asleep. "I can't believe you're hungry."

Silas kissed her hairline. "I worked it off. I think it's time for dessert."

He stretched, rolled out of her bed, and pulled his shorts on. Sofia rolled into his spot on the bed. "Don't get up now," he teased.

She followed him into the kitchen a moment later in a silk robe covered in huge printed poppies. She opened the freezer and pulled out an unlabeled bottle. The contents were pale yellow beneath the frost.

"Limoncello?" he asked.

"Mm hmm." Her eyes sparkled. A flush still lingered on her skin. "A friend of mine in DC makes her own. It's wonderful stuff."

Silas reached into a cabinet for two small glasses and poured them each a few sips.

They tucked into the lemon bars and toasted one another with the homemade liquor.

Silas raised his glass. "To your father, who might not have partaken, but I think would have approved."

Sofia's face clouded for a moment and he regretted inviting Jimmy's ghost into the room. Then she raised her own glass, pushing the moment aside.

"To my mother, who would have concluded such a meal with her own limoncello. I only wish I'd gotten to try it."

"To women of taste," Silas agreed, "and exceptionally good red sauce."

After their belated dessert, Sofia poured them a second round of limoncello and curled up on the sofa, patting the cushion next to her. He sat and she fit herself against his body. He leaned back, and snuggled her close. The noise from the street drifted through the open windows and the waves washed below like a slow heartbeat.

Silas woke a few hours later. The evening had cooled, and Sofia must have pulled the afghan from the end of the couch over them as they slept. Easing himself off the sofa, he slipped a pillow under Sofia's head and tucked the blanket snugly around her. He pushed her hair away from her face and kissed her, noting the soft hint of a smile on her lips.

SOFIA WOKE ALONE ON THE SOFA SOME TIME before dawn. When further sleep evaded her, she set about tidying up the apartment. Silas's record choices were still stacked on the console. She slipped the vinyl into their sleeves and carried them into her parents' room. The contents of the box Silas had emptied were in neat piles next to the carton.

It wasn't until she'd returned all the LPs to the box that she saw it. A shoebox from the mall store where she'd picked out her prom shoes, bought with the proceeds from her tips working the ice cream window, sealed with yellowed packing tape and her name, written on top in her own girlish script.

She carried the shoebox into her bedroom and slit the tape open with a nail file. By the light of her bedside lamp, she lifted the lid. Inside were snapshots of her with Judy, with Dex, hugging people she barely remembered, their fire-lit faces joyful against the indigo sea. There was a knotted friendship bracelet, faded by sun and seawater, snipped clean off her ankle at the end of a summer. Bits of polished glass, a sand dollar, a ticket stub from a carnival. At the bottom, a Florentine paper journal, tied closed with gros-grain ribbon.

Her diary.

The pages were crammed with the fluid, looping penmanship she'd long ago left behind, chronicling crushes and heartbreaks, kisses with boys whose lips she'd forgotten, fights with Judy, and secrets confided around those beach bonfires.

The pages also told the story of a girl who'd bled—figuratively—for her father's attention. A note in the margin with her GPA and a bitter scrawl: another girl's dad would have cared. The word "cared" underlined three times so hard the pen nip had almost broken through. A paragraph describing the night Judy's parents had taken them into Boston to celebrate their high school graduation. She wondered at the coincidence of eating her first formal dinner in the DeVarona Boston's dining room, Serenade.

While her father had been invited as a matter of form, he hadn't even bothered to decline.

She'd seen her first off-Broadway musical that night, had her first champagne toast in their hotel room, and cried her last bitter tears over her father in the bathroom.

From the dresser, her phone alarm chirped. With a heavy sigh, she pushed the diary into the box and shoved it under her bed. Until Kevin Landry brought her a buyer, she had obligations to fulfill.

Six

As the end of July melted into early August, Sofia boxed away more than just her diary. She allowed the pleasure of Silas's company to carry her through the dog days of a New England summer. They ran their respective businesses, slipping away when time warranted to be together away from the beach, and spending many of their nights tangled up in Sofia's bed.

Before too long, those nights outnumbered the nights they spent apart. The part of her that feared the intimacy that blossomed between them was stashed away under the bed with her box of memories.

On the cusp of a mid-August dawn, their phone alarms woke them at nearly the same moment. After a bleary shuffle to the living room, Silas tossed two silenced phones on the duvet and crawled back into the bed. What began as an easy good-morning kiss left them both breathless and aching, but Houdini was waiting for his breakfast, and the still empty beach was waiting for his run. Silas pushed Sofia's hair from her face and cruised his lips over her temple.

"Come to Portsmouth with me Sunday night." He kept his tone casual.

Indecision played over her face.

"Switch shifts with Amy." He traced her cheekbones with a finger and kissed her mouth. "She can close the course and the snack bar, and I'll have you home by midnight." He drew an x over her left breast. "Promise."

"Okay." She dodged him and rolled out of bed. Silas admired her behind as she walked away. "I saw that," she called from the kitchen.

He couldn't help laughing. She was magnificent. "Couldn't resist!"

He stepped into his boxers and padded out to the living room to find the rest of his clothes. In the adjoining kitchen, Sofia was making coffee.

"You should never make coffee with clothes on," he said.

She pushed start on the machine. "Smart ass."

He ogled. "Great ass."

"Help yourself to coffee. I'm going to grab a shower before I go down." She started for the bathroom.

He touched her arm as she passed. "Hey."

Her expression clouded and cleared in a blink.

"I've got to spend some time with my accounts tonight, but I'll be around." He kissed her and released her to her morning ablutions.

He grabbed a mug from the dish rack by the sink, poured a cup, and opened her fridge for some milk. Finding nothing suitable, he took the coffee, mug and all, out with him.

He arrived home to a very hungry cat. Scratching Houdini behind the ears, he headed for the jug of two-percent in his fridge, but his feline companion stopped him with a plaintive yowl and proceeded to wind himself around Silas's ankles.

"If you kill me, cat," he warned, "it could be days before anyone notices. You think you're hungry now?" Silas filled Houdini's bowls with kibble and water, and set the bowls down on the counter next to his coffee. "Let's you and me have some quality time."

FOR A DAY THAT BEGAN SO WELL, SOPHIA WAS almost impressed by how quickly it went bad. She was knee deep in the water feature, unclogging a filter, when Amy brought the phone out to her. Her soft-serve vendor was stuck in traffic. Later that morning, a couple of rowdy sports fans got into it over the Sox and the Yankees, and she'd ended up giving free rounds of golf to everyone whose games were interrupted.

Her tenants in 2B lost their key on the beach; the cable and internet went out. The annoyances were never-ending. By the time the sun set, she was dead on her feet.

Sofia locked up the golf course gates and switched off the sub-panel that controlled the lights, music, and water system. She could hear Charlotte teasing Gavin behind the counter of the snack bar while they cleaned up after what had been a very busy shift. Their adolescent sparring made her smile, despite a pounding headache. She'd wagered their banter would turn into a full-blown romance, and she'd been right. As long as it didn't interfere with the pouring of fountain drinks and the soft-serve machine operation, she was all in favor of their puppy-love.

Listening to them was a bittersweet reminder. Like her teenage employees, she'd cut her dating teeth behind that very window, but their awkward flirtation lodged behind her breastbone like a stone. No matter how many boys flirted back, no matter how much laughter rang through those seemingly endless days, she'd had to go home to a broken father and loneliness that carved out her heart. She couldn't help pitying Charlotte and Gavin a little. Like her stay in Hampton, such loves weren't destined to outlast the summer.

By the time Charlotte's father came to pick the pair up after work, Sofia's restless melancholy had settled in to stay. She changed into more comfortable clothes and sought solace on the cool, damp sand.

The beach never really slept in the summer. Even now, a little past midnight, the tide sneaking in quietly, the sand cool between her toes, there were others around. It had always been like that. The visitors came for the aging rock stars and comedians playing at the Casino, the fried dough stands, and the promise of the cold Atlantic water to soothe their ill-advised sunburns. But when the sun faded and the neon lights came on, Ocean Boulevard got a second wind, and those seeking a break from the hustle and jangle of the arcade and the crush of young people preening came down to the silvery beach.

Sofia chose her spot with some care, sitting on the slight rise above the high tide line. She gave a pair of young lovers some space, and kept far enough away from a group of kids with illicit sparklers to avoid trouble from the Beach Patrol. Before her mother had died, she'd been the instigator, begging her father to light sparklers and Roman candles off from the beach, dancing in the moonlit surf. Even her Dad had danced back then.

Her childhood curled in on the tide, crashing at her feet. She probed the memories tentatively. She'd had ten years to bury them, and bury them she had, but this place had been her home.

The winter was a different animal for a year-round resident of a summer vacation town. A mile inland life went on, autumn eased the transition from blistering summer to snowy chill, but here on the shoreline, there were fewer leaves to turn. The tourist season ended, the clam-shacks and pizza-by-the-slice counters shuttered. The quiet descended. Except for the few restaurants that stayed open to cater to the Casino Ballroom patrons, the strip went dormant.

When her mother's sunshine warmed those long, dark days by the shore, she hadn't noticed the cold. She'd gone merrily off to school every morning. Coming home in the afternoon to find her mother making homemade linguine or a big pot of Bolognese had banished a salty north wind. The second floor units were rented out to groups of UNH students in the off-season, usually trios or quartets of brave young guys willing to stick out the winter and the drive into Dover for classes in order to live cheap. Elena Costa Buck's cooking became something of an off-campus legend. If you rented at Buck's Landing, Mrs. Buck would cook for you a few times a week.

Those dinners had been spicy and rich in conversation —warm, cozy, boisterous meals. Even without their boarders, home was all music and laughter and warmth. Her mother's laugh was infectious, her beauty unmatched on the boulevard. Her Dad's rugged good looks and larger than life humor made life on the New Hampshire coastline an endless adventure. They'd been three against the world, a family.

A cold lick of seawater touched her toes, and Sofia realized the tide was fully in. She hitched up the hems of her wide-legged linen trousers. She was startled when Silas dropped down on the sand next to her.

"I used to catch your Dad down here from time to time. Same spot."

She didn't turn, didn't encourage him to stay. Childish though it might be, she wanted to be alone with her bad mood. "It's right across the street from the Landing. I suspect it's just convenient."

"I was taking care of a few things. I saw you come down here." He reached up to stroke her hair; a pleasant shiver ran down her back, but the onslaught of memories wouldn't let her go. When he spoke, he seemed to think she'd come down here to commune with her father's ghost. "I only knew your dad for a few months, but liked him a lot."

Grief swelled up. Anger formed a seawall to keep it at bay. Her quiet response belied the storm inside. "I haven't been home in ten years, Silas. I didn't even know him."

Silas slipped his shoes off and pulled them up next to him. He dug into the sand with his feet before folding his legs into a cross-legged position and reaching down to sift the beach through his fingers. "Your dad told me you used to like to fish."

His calm diffused some of her fury, and Sofia laughed bitterly. "I did. That was a long time ago."

"He said you were always riding your bike down to the lobster pounds and the sport-fishing places, hanging around the marinas. While it was okay to drop a line across the bridge, what you really wanted was to go out on a boat and fish."

"I've still never fished from a boat." Finding a smooth stone, she worried it between her fingers as the old longing for the open ocean swamped her. "There was never enough money when I was little, and after my mom... It just never happened."

"He said that he wanted to buy a Boston Whaler to take you out, but I sometimes wondered if he was talking about the little girl he lost, or the woman he didn't know anymore."

"He stopped caring." She fought fresh tears. "My mom died when I was eleven. She had a congenital heart defect. She just crumpled one day, while the marinara was cooking. Dad went from a guy who liked a can of High Life after dinner, or maybe a little glass of Mom's homemade limoncello, to a bottomless whiskey bottle of grief and bitterness. Did he tell you that?" She pulled her hand away. "I'm like her. You've seen the photos. Same skin, same dark eyes and hair. He couldn't bear to look at me because I reminded him that the love of his life was dead."

"Is that what you thought?"

"It's what I know!" Sofia pitched the stone into the surf. "What could you possibly know about it? You were my father's neighbor for half a year. He was a miserable drunk for half my childhood."

The outburst left her feeling exposed. Solitude no longer appealed. She leaned into Silas, craving his steadiness.

"Did I ever tell you how I met him?"

His voice rumbled under his skin where her cheek pressed against his shoulder. She shook her head slightly.

"The second day I was in town was a crazy warm day for January, maybe forty-five or fifty degrees and sunny. I walked up from the motel I was checked into on Ashworth and headed south along the shore."

Sofia pulled her knees up close to her chest to ward off the breeze. Silas went on with his story.

79

"I heard a saw, which seemed somehow out of place, so I walked up to the boardwalk to check it out. There was a guy—your dad—under the awning at Buck's Landing, with sawhorses and a table saw set up. He looked up and waved, just a casual greeting to a welcome stranger. That was when I saw the For Sale sign on the market building. I bought it that day." He scooped up a handful of sand. "In a way, your Dad led me to where I am. I didn't even see inside until I'd already made an offer."

Bitterness flooded her mouth like venom. Everyone was an expert on Jimmy Buck, but none of them had lived through her mother's death with the man. "I don't need your stories about how great he was, Silas. Like I said, I didn't even know that man. The one I knew wouldn't have welcomed a stranger. He didn't even welcome his own child."

"People change, Sofia."

The seawall around her emotions cracked, and the words poured through, hot and vicious. "My father drowned his grief in booze and let the business fall apart while he chased my mother's ghost through the house. I lost them both when she died. I spent six years figuring out how to get out of town, and then after college I left. I left and I never came back. I made a life for myself, goddammit. I left a job I worked my ass off to be the best at, a beautiful little condo in a neighborhood I like, to come here because my father had the unmitigated gall to die." A sob broke her voice.

A summer's worth of unshed tears spilled over. She pushed up, away from Silas and memories and unwanted sympathy, but his big, warm hand held her tight.

Desire and instinct warred within her. Her body ached for his touch, for the playful intimacy that had woven itself into the fabric of their days, but the violence of her emotions, the driving, white-hot rage her father's legacy brought out in her had finally surfaced, and she was terrified there was no turning back. Silas turned to her, eyes glittering in the reflected streetlight from the boardwalk. He had only wanted to comfort; it wasn't his fault that the heat between them was too much to resist. Desire won out. Her heart won out. She tucked up her trousers and settled uneasily on the sand, still trying to keep some distance between them. He reached for her anyway.

"What the hell are you doing?"

"Comforting you," he said, sliding his hand up her arm.

HE SAW IT IN HER EYES, THE BATTLE BETWEEN fight and flight. He told himself he was ready for either one. Then he caught it, the slightest softening.

"I don't need comforting." Her words didn't match the husky delivery.

He stretched up, stroked her cheek, his other hand still resting just above her elbow. Her body was strung tight. "Of course you don't."

So easy to slide his fingers into all that silky, dark hair. So easy to draw her face in close. She smelled like the cool sand, like salt and summer air, but underneath was something more complex. Searching out the source, he whispered over her jaw line and inhaled the fragrance of the fine skin behind her ear. Perfume, fresh and floral, but musky, and then underneath that, a spicy note that he knew to be all her own. He inhaled again, this time pressing his lips to taste the smooth column of her throat.

An audible sigh escaped her lips, and she turned into him.

He'd once heard that drowning was a pleasant way to die, that the mind slipped into bliss in the final moments. It had always seemed far-fetched to him, but when her lips sought his out in the darkness, when her hair and her scent closed out the percussion of the coming tide, when the air he breathed thickened like water in his lungs, he understood. This was drowning and it was bliss.

He shifted, tested the depth of contact. She yielded; the kiss turned him over and he lost himself. He'd expected to spar with her; the tenderness that washed over him left him defenseless. Her lips parted against his, her hands drifted up to press against his chest, but not in protest. From his chest, up and around his neck, her fingers searched out his bare skin. The taste of her pulled him in.

Her tongue teased his lips, tangled with his, even as she melted against him, rocking him into the sand. His hands coasted down her back, pulling her close with a growl of pleasure. Her skin, exposed between the tank she wore under the flimsy wrap and her linen pants, was warm under his palms and he wanted more, but she was pushing away, scrambling for purchase in the loose sand.

For the second time that night, Silas followed her. A few months of morning runs on the beach gave him the advantage. Grabbing his sneakers, he loped off after her over the manmade dunes. He caught up with her before she'd gone very far, just where the beach parking lot ended at Haverhill Avenue.

"Please, Sofia. Don't push me away."

She whirled on him, fire in her eyes, moonlight on her skin.

There was none of the melting tenderness of before.

This kiss scorched, burned. Her mouth was hot and insistent on his. He should have been offended, or at least turned off, by her hot and cold routine, but she was winding her hands up in his shirt and hauling him up against her body. He was helpless to resist.

"Sofia," he whispered against her lips. "I want you."

"Yes." Her reply was almost a whimper.

Not one to waste an opportunity, he angled his lips and plundered. He took her invitation, exploring her with tongue and teeth, wrapping her in his arms, filling his senses with her. Even her flavor was ice and fire. He slid his hands up under her top; the muscles of her back flexed beneath his palms as she stretched up and closer. He circled her ribcage with his fingers, brushing satin and lace, teasing the underside of her breasts.

He forced himself to break the kiss. They were bordering on public indecency. He chuckled, still breathing hard.

"Upstairs?"

They made it as far as her landing, but he was part of the fire now, burning as hot as she did. She moaned and pressed herself against the door, hips jangling the keys in the lock. Silas leaned in, one hand slipping between her bra and the softness of her flesh, the other cupping her ass and pulling her up tight against him. She could have no illusions about how much he wanted her. Pushing the wrap from Sofia's shoulders, drawing her camisole up, he brushed her nipple with his thumb. She gasped, sighed, shoved at the waistband of his jeans.

He reached for the doorknob, and they stumbled together through the door.

SOFIA'S ANGER WAS GONE, BURNED TO ASH IN THE passion that flamed between them. Her body screamed for release.

Silas backed her up against the counter, deftly undid the catch at the waist of her linen trousers. The air on her bare legs as the linen pooled raised gooseflesh; his warm hands chased the chill away. He lifted her up, settling himself between her thighs.

She kissed him, tugging at his bottom lip with her teeth while she worked his tee shirt up over his head. Clothing dropped around them as they devoured one another.

She reached for him, guiding him to her, wrapping her body around him. Sofia held him there, hardly daring to move, lest the breathless moment end. Then they were moving together, streaking towards the edge, hurling themselves over.

Sofia held on to Silas while he caught his breath, loathe to let him go.

He laid his head against her breast. "Hey."

"Yeah." She smiled, resting her cheek on the top of his head.

"Are you okay?" He raised his face to look into her eyes.

She laughed lightly, aftershocks still shivering through her muscles. "I'm tougher than I look."

Silas kissed her. "I know that. Seriously," he searched her eyes again, "you're all right?"

She brushed a long lock of fair hair away from his face. "I'm okay."

"I'd like to stay, but I left some lights on and I need to check on the cat monster."

"Come back soon," she said, hopping down from the counter to turn on the light for the landing and help him find his clothes.

The door had barely closed behind him when her phone trilled from the pocket of her discarded pants.

Rubbing her temple, she pulled it out. Blinking in surprise, she connected the call.

"Elliot." She closed her eyes a moment, trying to place the last time they'd spoken. "I thought you were still...away."

"Unexpected detour." His voice was brisk but warm, with the faint hint of Europe that he cultivated despite being from an upscale suburb of Chicago. "I'm in Boston."

Her heart skipped uneasily. "Really?"

She heard a series of digital beeps. "My GPS tells me you're only an hour away."

She heard the suggestion behind his words, and chose to ignore it. There was no point in encouraging him. "How long are you in town?"

"I'm heading down to Washington tomorrow night, then I have a meeting in Beijing."

"A meeting?" She knew he was speaking in riddles on purpose, but she was used to his cloak and dagger.

"Is there room for me in your twin bed?"

"It's not a twin bed." The defensive tone of her own voice caught her off guard. He'd done nothing wrong, but his intrusion irked.

At the beginning of the summer, she would have told him to meet her at one of the inns along the coast between there and Boston. The spontaneity would have made them hungrier for one another. Now, she could only think of Silas, on his way back up any minute. "Trust me, Elliot. You'd hate it up here."

"Bit primitive?" Even his affected speech grated on her remaining nerves.

"Something like that." She switched the phone to her

other ear and pressed her fingers hard into her temple. "I'll be in D.C. sometime in September. Maybe we can meet up then?"

His reply was considerably cooler. "Perhaps."

"Look, Elliot." Irritation got the better of her. "It's not a good time. I'm so glad you called, and I'm sorry I can't drop everything to be with you, but I can't. Please don't make this more than it is."

The brief silence on the other end of the line was telling.

"No, Sofia. I won't do that."

"Elliot..." She didn't really know what to say.

He saved her the trouble. "Call me when you're home. We'll catch up then."

Elliot ended the call. Sofia laid her phone down on the counter.

Silas was true to his word. She watched his lights wink out in his apartment and met him at her door with an affectionate kiss. Falling back on the rhythm of their nights together, they stretched out on her bed with the heavy night air over them like a blanket. Silas's deep, untroubled breathing came quickly. Sleep evaded her, so she slipped out of bed.

A glance at the clock told her it was far too late to be up. The garbage pick-ups would come too soon, and she no longer had a child's ability to sleep through the racket. She paused at her parents' bedroom door. As in her own bedroom, her father had framed half a dozen fading photographs of their little family, clustering them on the dresser. From the doorway she could see her mother smiling over the stove, the three of them by an enormous, scraggly Christmas tree, and her smaller self, walking ahead of the lens, carrying her fishing pole over her tanned and freckled shoulder. Cutoffs, filthy Keds, and a Kermit the Frog tee shirt all just a hint too small. Her mother would have been saving for back-to-school clothes.

She thought of the bookshelf in her apartment in D.C. Photos of her summer camp "sisters," her college friends, a recent ski trip to Lake Tahoe with a few friends from her work life, a bachelorette party in Las Vegas. It was almost as though there were two of her, the happy little girl and the satisfied woman.

The years between were the ones missing from the collage. Her thoughts strayed to the shoebox under her bed full of that teenage girl's memories. Her father didn't have those photographs; she'd left them sealed away when she escaped. She thought she'd made a clean split from that broken girl.

She knew the truth now. The split was anything but clean. The wound was ragged, the scar tissue lumpy and disfigured. She'd assumed it was past reopening, but in her deepest heart she'd also assumed there would be time to reconcile with her father on her own terms. Instead, his memory was held by a man with a charming smile and an appealing steadiness, a man who insisted on sharing it with her when all she wanted to do was forget.

When she went back to bed, it was to an uneasy sleep, pursued by dreams of gray kittens, fishing rods, and the smell of marinara.

Seven

Uneasy sleep gave way to an uneasy day. Storm clouds threatened the coast, which left the Landing with fewer customers. Without a steady stream of business, Sofia took herself out to inspect the course. Sprucing it up would improve her chances of selling quickly and closer to her asking price.

The replica of the Piscataqua Bridge on the first tee needed some touch-up paint. She thought of the real bridge, the crossing to Maine. With a sigh, she realized she'd been in town almost two months and hadn't driven up to Portland or even over to Kittery to hit the outlet stores. Once the papers were signed, it wouldn't matter. She'd be heading south again.

The Sphinx on the fourth hole, to whose open mouth a ramp rose, had a few divots in the concrete that needed patching. The promotion to Luxelle was nearly in her grasp. This time next year, Egypt might just be a jaunt across the Mediterranean.

The tree on the twelfth hole needed another bleaching. The shade and the proximity to the water feature left it perpetually mildewed. There were faint scratches on the trunk from its run in with Houdini. Her thoughts strayed again to Silas.

So often when they were together, she forgot her hurt and anxiety, forgot that selling Buck's Landing was the endgame. She let herself drift with the summer current, enjoying Silas's company. He made her laugh; he smoothed her rough edges. He walked an unsullied world, unshadowed by dark memories. She reveled in the pleasure they found together. Even when it came to the two of them, he was sure about where he stood. Far more so than she was about herself.

Elliot's call had been a splash of cold water after the heat of the evening's emotions and passion. Silas had left early for his morning run; she'd barely been able to lift her head from the pillow after too little sleep.

She looked at a few more of the putting greens, but her head simply wasn't in the game. She checked the time on her phone. Amy would be in to cover the evening shift shortly. The day's meager take would need to be tallied before Sofia turned the register over. She only just made it to the cashier window before the sky opened, followed by gusty winds. A menace of thunderheads gathered to the southwest while the rain blew sideways over the Astroturf.

Amy raced in a short while later, soaked from the rain, a telltale splatter of muddy water on the backs of her legs.

"Oh, no." Sofia grabbed the nearby paper towel roll. "You rode your bike in."

The young woman shucked her sopping sweatshirt and hung it up. "I thought I could beat the worst of it."

"Come on upstairs," Sofia offered. "Let me lend you some dry clothes."

Amy mopped her face and wrung out her ponytail with her wet shirt. "Sure. Thanks."

Sofia put up the sign redirecting customers to the ice cream window and called to Gavin that she and Amy were going up. They ran out the back and up the stairs to the apartment. Sofia grabbed a towel from the bathroom, and tossed it on her bed with a pair of her shorts and one of the Buck's Landing staff shirts she'd claimed from her father's closet. She found Amy smiling at an old family photo on the mantle.

"There's a towel and dry things on the bed."

Amy turned around, blushing. "I'm sorry. I wasn't snooping. Your mother was beautiful. You look like her."

"Thank you." Sofia went to the fridge to avoid Amy's earnest expression.

Amy came out a few moments later holding the towel. Sofia took it. "I poured you some iced tea."

"Thanks." Amy stuffed her empty hand in her pocket. The awkward silence stretched until the younger woman spoke. "I love that fuchsia dress."

Sofia had forgotten about the dress, hung up on her closet door in anticipation of her evening out. She grinned, the awkwardness diffused by fashion. "I bought it on a whim a few weeks ago up in Portsmouth. That little shop up the road from The Lunch Counter."

"'Fête?" Amy lit up. "I love that store."

"I was going to wear it to dinner at Orionis on Sunday." She wished she had experience with sisters. Was she over sharing?

Amy spoke, interrupting her doubts. "With Mr. Wilde?"

"Yeah." Sofia felt a flush burn her cheeks. Amy looked

away quickly. Sofia put a hand on the younger woman's shoulder. "What's wrong?"

"Nothing," Amy reassured her.

If there was one thing Sofia understood, it was false brightness.

"Pardon my French," she said, "but bullshit."

Amy's chin quivered. Sofia pushed down some guilt. She didn't know the girl well enough to bully a confession out of her, and she'd never had a sister to trade advice with, just girlfriends, all of them together in the trenches of whatever youthful misery was en vogue. As she'd said to Judy, she kind of sucked at confiding.

"It's just stupid guy stuff," Amy muttered.

Sofia had a sudden urge to demand the offending male's name before marching off to drag him back by his scruff to beg forgiveness. She hated that some boy had the power to take the shine off her favorite employee.

Instead, she settled in to hear the young woman out. "I can be a good listener."

"I've been kind of seeing this guy this year," she began.

Sofia hopped up on a counter, settling in for the long haul.

"He told me this afternoon that he thinks we should break up." Amy swiped at her eyes. "We drove up to Kittery to pick out some stuff for my apartment in the fall, and he was all, 'I don't think long-distance will work for us, so why are we wasting the summer?'"

Sofia let out a breath, while Amy went on. There was no point interrupting.

"How is having a great summer together before I go wasting it?" she asked. "If he doesn't want to be with me after, I get it, but why can't we keep going 'til I leave?"

Her tears spilled over just as the rain outside began to let up. Sofia handed Amy a tissue.

"I got a text from one of my friends. She saw him at the movies just now with a bunch of people, and there was some skanky girl hanging all over him. I feel really stupid." Amy blew her nose wetly.

Sofia handed her another tissue. She'd dated, certainly, in high school, and fooled around her fair share in college, but she'd never allowed herself to get close, to get serious, about any boy from the area. She hadn't been interested in tying herself to Hampton, knowing she planned to run and never look back.

"I know this is going to sound like a platitude," Sofia said gently, "but maybe it's for the best."

Amy looked at her wide-eyed.

"You're off to New Haven, to a graduate degree at Yale in the fall, and he's off to..." She trailed off, realizing she had no idea if Amy's boyfriend was going anywhere.

"He's not going anywhere," she said quietly. "He works in Manchester."

"Oh, Amy," she said. "You don't want to be tied to home. You're going to meet people, men, from all over, and then after school, the whole world. I know it hurts now." She collected the tissues and dropped them in the trash basket under the kitchen sink. "But you'll be free of this place in just a few weeks, really."

"Free from Hampton? Why would I want that?" Amy asked.

Sofia recalled the pressing weight of her own need to escape. "Don't you want to travel, to live? Can't you feel the world at your feet right now?"

"Hampton is my home. My family's here. I grew up here, just like you. I'll always be tied to this place. I want to be ready to fight for the beach, to keep the town from overdeveloping, to make sure the old businesses don't all fade away." Her face was ablaze with earnest energy. "Like you are with the Landing. Third generation Buck to own it, my mom says."

Sofia felt her soul shrivel a little, a dark, brooding heaviness in her chest.

"Look, Amy, you feel that way now—"

"I'm getting my Masters in Environmental Management so I can come back to the seacoast, Sofia. I've always wanted that." She sat up straighter. Sofia recognized the soapbox of youthful enthusiasm coming out. "What you're doing here, cleaning the place up, making it more of a showpiece? I want to work with owners like you to revitalize the strip without damaging the actual land any more than it is, you know?"

"You'll be amazing." Sofia gazed at Amy's idealistic glow. Her tears forgotten, she pulsed with dreams. "I'm sorry I won't be here to see it."

"What do you mean?" Amy's glow faltered.

"I never meant to stay on at the Landing for good." Some of the heaviness in her chest cracked apart. "I've listed it with Kevin Landry's office up in Portsmouth."

"Listed it?" Amy's eyes went wide. "Not for development?"

Sofia swallowed the urge to snap at Amy. "For whatever purpose the new owner sees fit, within the zoning laws."

"Oh." The flat look that crept across the girl's face turned Sofia's stomach. She let anger have the moment.

"Did you really think I was here to stay?" She snapped her fingers. "Just like that?"

"I don't know what I thought." Amy squared her shoulders. "It's really none of my business, anyway."

Sofia had the uncomfortable sensation of being dismissed in her own apartment. She pulled out her phone to check the time. "You should head down. Gavin won't be able to handle too much business on his own."

Amy's cheeks stained. "Listen, Sofia," she said, "I was out of line, and I'm sorry. I get a little carried away sometimes."

"You made a strong point," Sofia conceded, "and I reacted badly." Better to smooth things over with her favorite employee. "Don't worry about it."

"Well," Amy said, with none of her earlier frosty disapproval, "I should get to work. Thanks for the clothes."

———

SILAS'S PHONE BUZZED FROM HIS POCKET, BUT HE was closing out the registers, so he let the call go to voicemail. With the majority of the day's take locked away, he felt safer leaving Theo in charge of closing the store. His nephew claimed to enjoy his late shifts, since he'd started hanging around one of the midway hawkers whose shifts ended late, too. She had violet hair, favored snug tops and short shorts, and was an American History major at Harvard who preferred the noise on the strip to an air-conditioned research internship.

To Silas's horror, she referred to him as Mr. Wilde. He couldn't decide if Mallory would love the girl or hate her.

Speaking of the devil, Mallory's name popped up on his missed call alert. He tapped her name and listened to the ring.

"Silas."

He could hear the smile in his sister's voice. He could also hear the gears turning. "Mal. What's up?"

"I was just calling to check on my son."

Silas chuckled. "No. You talked to him on his dinner break."

"Fine." Mallory sighed. "I just wanted to know if there was anything more with that girl."

"His?" Silas teased. "Or mine?"

"Yours. Of course. My son doesn't associate with girls."

"That girl is my age." He pushed the cash drawer closed and waved the deposit bag at Theo. "Don't make me sound like some dirty old man."

"Well, at least she's not my age. Can't have you bagged by some cougar."

"Okay, seriously?" Silas laughed. "She could be older than I am, but I don't think she's in her fifties yet." He braced for screaming.

"Forty, smart boy; I am forty. I ought to write you out of my will for that."

"Yeah?" Upstairs, he unlocked his safe, and deposited the bag inside for the night. "You planning on leaving me the kid?"

"Wait," she teased, "I take it back. I think Ted and I are both going to fake our deaths so you have put him through three more years of college."

Silas grabbed a beer from the fridge and popped the top. Houdini slept, sprawled among a pile of disemboweled catnip mice, his round kitten belly rising and falling with the peace of a contented creature.

"Good plan." He sat in a ratty thrift store armchair he'd rescued. The sun was just beginning to sink, tinting the light that fell on Buck's Landing a rosy gold. His gaze fell on the gauzy sweater he'd peeled from Sofia's shoulders the night before. In his haste to get her out of her clothes, the wrap must have fallen over the railing, landing at the bottom of the stairs. He'd nearly slipped on it that morning leaving her apartment. She'd barely been able to lift her head to kiss him goodbye; he wasn't about to knock on her door again. Bringing it inside to return to her later seemed the chivalrous thing to do. "I'm sure Theo will love community college and slaving for his slacker uncle Silas."

"You're avoiding the question." Mallory wasn't relenting.

"What question is that?" he asked innocently.

"What's going on with that woman?"

Silas picked up the beer. "We got married in Niagara Falls last night." He helped himself a healthy swallow.

"Okay, fine," Mallory said. "I'll let you off the hook. For now."

He could picture her indulgent grin. "I love you, Mallory."

"I love you, too."

Silas ended the call and left his phone on the arm of the chair, finishing the beer in two swallows. He grabbed Sofia's sweater and headed next door to return it to her.

He heard Sofia before he got to the top of her stairs.

"I'm sorry I won't be here to see it."

"What do you mean?" Amy.

Sofia. "I never meant to stay on at the Landing for good." A pause. "I've listed it with Kevin Landry's office up in Portsmouth."

"Listed it?" Amy. "Not for development?"

Sofia, a little angry now. "For whatever purpose the new owner sees fit, within the zoning laws."

"Oh." Amy.

"Did you really think I was here to stay?" A snap of fingers. "Just like that?"

"I don't know what I thought." Amy trying for digni-fied. "It's really none of my business, anyway."

In the uncomfortable silence which followed, Silas processed what he'd heard. Not only did she not plan on staying past the season, she was going to sell Jimmy's legacy to god-knows-who and waltz back down to D.C. with some cash in hand and the freedom to bury her father's memory so deep it might never surface again.

He realized he was clenching the sweater. Her casual dismissal of Hampton, and by extension what was happening between them, bothered him. She belonged more than she was willing to see.

Or did he just want her to?

When the conversation between the two women inside resumed, he felt strange about loitering. Still carrying Sofia's sweater, he returned to the boulevard, taking a two street circular detour on his way home. He needed time to think.

Eight

Late Sunday afternoon Silas pulled the Jeep up outside the snack bar, waved at Gavin, and jogged up the stairs.

Sofia opened the door as he reached the landing. Her shoulders were bare, save for two slim straps, and while the deep pink of her dress covered the rest of her, it did nothing to hide the curves and hollows of her body. Her hair hung loose down her back in a curly riot. She shimmered. Her Mona Lisa smile confirmed it; she was secure in the knowledge that she had stolen his breath. He seriously considered scrapping their plans to drive up to Portsmouth in favor of tossing her over his shoulder and heading for the nearest soft surface.

The day before, he'd avoided her, pleading office work and Theo's day off. He'd hoped for perspective and clarity. He'd ended up not really caring that she planned to run again; he'd just wanted to be with her.

"I missed you." She was aglow. "Hold this."

He blinked, taking her purse from her outstretched

hand. She dashed into the apartment, returning a moment later with a dragonfly printed scarf trailing from her hand.

"Much better," she said, taking her bag.

Silas nodded and gestured ahead. "Milady."

Rolling her eyes, Sofia turned the key in the lock and led him down the stairs. She climbed into the Jeep and took a moment to tie her hair back with the scarf. She gave him a sidelong smile. "The better to enjoy going topless."

He was helpless against the barrage of images she evoked; she giggled at his obvious distress.

When he parked the car on State Street, she tied her scarf to the rearview mirror, shook out her hair, and joined him on the sidewalk. Something about the dragonfly printed silk fluttering against his dashboard squeezed his chest.

Orionis boasted only a dozen tables in a stone basement accessed from Ceres Street. The atmosphere inside was intimate, alive with Portsmouth's long seafaring history. Tucked into a shadowy corner under a copper lampshade, she swore she could hear the whispers of smugglers and patriots in the air. The menu was *avant gard*, the wine list extensive.

"May I?" Sofia took the wine list and began to peruse.

Silas wondered if she was aware that she chewed her lip when she concentrated.

"How do you feel about a bottle with dinner?" She tapped one short fingernail on a label name.

"I trust you."

Their server arrived and took their cocktail orders. He watched Sofia make short work of the menu, while he agonized over the choices.

His gin and tonic and her Moscow Mule arrived, and they traded menus for empty space. Sofia ordered the bottle of Spanish Garnacha with a knowing glance at the list. The sophisticated side of her only intrigued him more. He reached over to touch her hand on the table.

"You're beautiful," he said. "Have I told you that in the last five minutes?"

She laughed. "Not since you parked the car." She looked around at the brick walls and low light. "How did you find this place? It's wonderful."

"My sister found it. She and her husband had dinner up here when they brought Theo up for the summer." Silas stroked the web of soft skin between her thumb and forefinger. "She's one of those women who just find these places."

Sofia smiled smugly. "So am I."

"She'll love you," he said. His brow wrinkled. "Or she'll hate you."

Sofia pulled her hand away, and he instantly regretted the casual mention of his sister. Mallory would love Sofia; of that he was sure. The trick was going to be getting Sofia to stick around long enough to love Mallory. To love him.

And there it was. She was prickly, terrified, and complicated, and he was falling in love. She was like a riptide. She'd swept his feet out from under him, tumbled him over, and stolen his breath. She might still break him and toss him ashore.

The first course arrived, along with the wine, and there was no room at the table for his worries. Over dinner he told her about growing up in New Jersey, about his time at Princeton and his adventures as a law student at NYU.

"I thought it was all going to be like that," he mused over dinner. "I lived with some guys I knew. We were all in graduate school straight out of college, and when we weren't working or studying, it was like a buddy movie."

He poured the last of their wine.

"After school, though, the apartment broke up, I guess. We all went different ways, and I ended up living with another first-year associate from the firm. We weren't really friends; we both worked all the time, and I forgot how to enjoy my life."

Sofia took advantage of the pause. "When did you graduate from NYU?"

"Five years ago."

"You know, I was in New York around the same time." She counted back on her fingers. "My first job for DeVarona was at their midtown property. I was an assistant catering manager." She pursed her lips. "Of course, I'd been out of school for six years."

He did the math in his head. Three years. It was nothing, but Mallory would—quite cheerfully—never let him hear the end of it. He steered the conversation away from age.

"So, instead of slaving away for Stern & Lowe, I could have been taking you out for ridiculously overpriced sushi?"

Sofia nodded. "I do like sushi."

The check came while they were still discussing the gustatory pleasures of Manhattan. Outside, a light wind blew down the Piscataqua River bound for the Atlantic, chilling the waterfront. Sofia produced a cardigan sweater from her bag.

"I'm impressed." Silas eyed her bag suspiciously. It didn't seem big enough to hold a wardrobe change. He snuck a look at her shoes peeking out from under the long hem of her dress. "Are you up to a walk?"

"Not all the way back to Hampton," she laughed, "but around Portsmouth sounds good."

Silas took her hand. Silent surprise flitted across her face when he led her away from the brighter, busier streets. They passed the Strawberry Banke Museum, taking a quieter, darker route.

"Are we going to the park?" she asked, after a block or two.

"Nope."

"Are you going to tell me where we're going?" She sounded curious, but unconcerned.

He squeezed her hand. "I'll tell you, if you don't want it to be a surprise."

She stopped, eyes sparkling. "I don't want to ruin the surprise." She tipped her head. "But I do want to know."

His reply was soft. "Another block or so."

***

SOFIA WASN'T SURE WHERE SILAS WAS TAKING her, but under the teasing, she sensed something tentative in his body language. When they rounded the last corner before Portsmouth spilled out into the Harbor, she saw a faded, carved sign for Beaudette's Marina.

"An evening cruise?" she said.

"If you like, but not exactly." His response was pensive. He was counting the slips, looking for a particular boat. She followed him down to the docks.

He stopped in front of a shabby Boston Whaler. The small sport fishing boat looked mostly unused. Silas was watching her carefully. Sofia looked over the boat for some significance.

She almost missed it.

Stenciled along the side of the boat near the stern was a name. She wondered briefly what kind of sentimental fool named a tiny Boston Whaler, and then she read the name.

Elena Sofia.

Tears sprang up in her eyes; confusion welled in her chest. "I don't understand."

"She was your dad's." Silas pocketed his hands and looked out towards the horizon.

"I would have known about it. I've been through his will; the estate was in probate..." She frowned at Silas, who stayed silent, watching the Atlantic. Elena Sofia. Her father had bought a fishing boat and named it for her mother. For her. "How?"

Silas stepped aboard the Whaler and reached out for her. "You remember I told you how he talked to me about how you used to want to go fishing?"

She took the hand he offered and joined him. The boat bobbed a little on the water. Silas pulled out a flotation cushion and set it down for her to sit on. He sat facing her on the fiberglass deck.

"He asked me for help," Silas began. "I don't think he liked doing it, but he did. He asked me for a loan. He said that even if you never came home, he wanted to do something for you."

"Silas, I haven't fished since I was a kid."

"I know." He held up a hand to hush her. "He figured that, too, but he didn't know what else to do. He was afraid to push you, to contact you. He didn't want to hear you say you didn't want him."

Her breath caught.

Silas went on. "He talked a lot about that. How he could just pretend you had been away a long time, but you'd be back."

She could feel her chin quiver; feel the sting of tears in her nose. Silas's face blurred into the motion of the sea behind him.

"I bought the boat. I rented the slip." He paused to let her process the information. "We had a gentleman's agreement, I guess. He was going to pay me back."

"You'd known him how long, and you bought him a boat?" Her voice was thick, conflicting emotions choking her.

"I didn't need to know him a long time." He picked up the hem of her skirt where it pooled around her crossed ankles, rubbing the material between finger and thumb. "I trusted him. I trust my instincts about people."

Silas's instincts about her were so wrong. She wasn't at all who he thought she was. How could she tell him she was looking for a buyer?

"Why did you bring me here?" She forced down a sob. "Am I supposed to buy the boat from you to repay my father's debt?"

Silas dropped the hem of her dress. His eyes flashed dangerously. "Damn it, Sofia! This isn't about money, or debts, or me, for chrissake."

She pulled her knees up, hugging them while he lost his temper.

"I brought you here to show you, to give you some kind of tangible proof that he was trying." He raked his hair through with his hands and got awkwardly to his feet. "I brought you here because your father would have wanted me to. He would have wanted to. He would have been scared to death you'd reject him. He would have accepted it if you did. But he would have wanted you to see that he loved you."

The scream rose up before she could temper it. "You barely knew him. How could you know that?"

The dam burst. The tears streamed, her throat closed up with sticky, hot rage. She clung to her own body to ride out the storm. The keening wails were her own, she knew, but the wild creature that was her grief became something separate. Her whole body ached when the crying jag finally began to subside. She became aware of Silas, kneeling next to her, his hands warm on her shoulders. He pressed a bandanna into her fisted hand. She imagined it wasn't going to save her face, but she blew her nose and wiped away the worst of the dampness on her cheeks.

Very gently, Silas raised her chin and met her eyes. "I don't have to know someone for very long to know they mean a great deal to me."

"Don't." She shook her head slightly. "Don't say that."

After a beat of silence, Silas pushed up to his feet, helping her up and off the boat. "We should head back."

BACK IN HAMPTON, THE NIGHTLY PARTY ON Ocean Boulevard was only getting started. Silas parked the car and walked her to the stairs leading up to her apartment. He'd stayed largely silent on the half hour drive down I-95 and Route 101. Sofia's thoughts whirled, unable to fully accept the truth of Silas's gesture or the deeper truth it represented.

He stopped her at the stairs. "I'm sorry."

She started to halt his apology, but he continued on.

"I shouldn't have sprung the boat on you like that. I wanted tonight to end differently." He pushed a stray hair behind one ear, and traced the line where her scarf held the rest back, still bound from their drive.

"Yeah?" The word wobbled, as did her smile.

"Yeah." He pushed the scarf down, freeing her hair.

Sofia sucked in a breath. "I think I wanted that, too."

"Yeah?" He smiled, angling his mouth until his lips were a whisper from hers.

"Yeah." She closed her eyes, tired from weeping, and leaned into the kiss.

At first, he only sampled. Then his tongue was teasing hers, their tangled flavors salty with sadness, still tannic from the wine with dinner, and she forgot to think. She drifted into him, hands splayed out on his broad shoulders, body pressed close to his. He wrapped his arms around her and held on as he deepened the kiss, tucking them both into the shadows at the bottom of the stairs.

Hazy with pleasure, Sofia surrendered to the texture of the moment. The boisterous noise of the boardwalk a hum in her ears, the bass from passing cars pounding in her blood, the clean scent of Silas's soap mingling with the thick boardwalk air. His fair stubble rasped her lips. She threaded her hands into the warm hair at the back of his neck and stretched up to meet him as he nibbled his way along her jaw to her ear.

"Come up to my place."

His breath against the thin skin behind her ear sent sparks cascading along her body. "Yes." It was as much of a reply as she could muster.

He wasted no time. In a move Rhett Butler would have envied, he scooped her up under her knees and carried her around the fence, inside, and up the stairs to his apartment. He set her down on the doormat and unlocked the door. Houdini met them inside, purring and meowing with a purely feline blend of joy and annoyance.

Silas held her wrists and walked backward, leading her to his bedroom. The cat followed, squeaking with indignation when Silas shut the door. "Not tonight, cat."

Sofia had a heartbeat to take in the sparse decor. She

had an impression of a showroom floor bedroom set and department store linens before Silas tugged her down onto the bed and covered her body with his own. His eyes glittered in the dark.

"You are amazing."

For the second time that night, her breath caught. Silas reached down to slide the hem of her dress up and over her knee, and followed its descent down her thigh with his mouth. He raised her dress up and over the other knee, caressing the soft, lean flesh of her leg from ankle to hip.

Hooking her feet around him, she drew him closer to undo the row of buttons that marched down his shirt. He busied himself with the slim straps over her shoulder. Silas freed her breasts from the bodice of the dress. His fingers were feather-light, his mouth hot when he scraped nipping teeth over their sensitive tips. Piece by piece, they bared skin with hungry hands and lips. The night stretched out like taffy, time bending to fit their languid exploration. The same breeze that had chilled them in the marina cooled the flush of desire.

She stroked him, his obvious desire heavy against her palm. He groaned against her mouth when she rolled him underneath her, taking him in, bracing her hands on his chest, and bringing them both spiraling up further, higher, lost in each other until reason broke apart around them.

Silas drew her down, whispering into the indigo shadows. "Stay?"

Sofia nodded, heavy-lidded, and snuggled against him. He pulled a sheet up over them to ward off the breeze, and she slipped into a deep, contented sleep.

She woke to an unfamiliar bar of sunlight and contented feline rumbling in her ear. When Houdini stretched, flexing his paws in her tangled hair, she laughed.

She'd fallen asleep with the man and woken up with his cat. Blinking, she scrubbed the sleep from her eyes. Silas's apartment was empty, but the clock revealed that she hadn't overslept. Rolling out of bed, she tugged the fuchsia dress over her head.

She padded into the kitchen with Houdini at her heels. On the brown laminate counters was a Stern & Lowe New York mug next to a pricey grind-and-brew machine. A note in tidy block print instructed her to help herself to the coffee. She touched the stainless steel carafe. Still warm. She poured and leaned against the counter, watching the end of the sunrise over the nearly empty beach.

The cat rubbed up against her calves, brushing the dress's fabric out along his tail. Silas's teasing echoed in her memory.

"You should never make coffee with clothes on."

She wondered if he'd made the coffee before he dressed for his dawn run. Out the window, she watched a jogger make his way barefoot along the high tide line. He ran easy, she thought. His body flowed over the sand, without tension or rush. It wasn't until he shifted his stride to cross the softer sand that she realized it was Silas. Houdini leapt up to the counter and helped himself to some spilled coffee. She scratched him behind his ears.

"Classy animal."

Houdini purred in reply.

Silas rinsed his feet off at the shower stands; his wet feet left fading footprints as he crossed the beach parking lot and the street. Sofia swallowed the last of her coffee and rinsed the mug in the sink. She was at the door to the bedroom to collect the rest of her clothes when Silas came in.

He swung her around by the waist to face him, greeting

her with a kiss tasting of salt and adrenaline. "Good morning."

"Hi," was all Sofia could manage before he was kissing her again, smoothing the dress over her ribcage, dipping his hands into the bodice to touch her breasts, bending to take her nipples into his mouth, one tight peak then another. When she peeled his shirt over his head, his skin was hot to the touch under a sheen of clean sweat peppered with fine sand.

Suddenly impatient, she pushed her dress down, shimmying it over her hips. Silas slipped out of his running shorts, watching her undress with a hungry gaze. Reaching for her, he kissed her again. Her head spun with lust and caffeine. He steered them not to the bedroom, but to the adjoining bath.

"Silas?"

"I'm filthy." His smile was wicked. "I really need a shower."

Nine

E ven with the shower, Sofia was still early to work. Amy found her touching up the paint on the Old Man of the Mountain who looked down on the eighteenth green. She had Sofia's phone in hand.

"Morning, Sofia." She handed over the phone. "This was ringing when I signed the timesheet."

Sofia checked her missed calls. "Thanks, Amy. Do you want to open the register or take over for me out here?"

"I'll take over out here, if that's okay."

Sofia opened her voicemail on the way back to the office. The missed call was from Judy.

Sof, it's Judy. Keep Saturday open. We're having a cookout around four and it's about damn time you met Christopher and the kids. Bring dessert and Silas. Don't worry, we'll be nice. See you then.

She texted Silas, thinking as she did so that they rarely, if ever, used their phones. The habit of wandering between their two buildings in search of one another had formed easily. Maybe too easily. Her phone pinged. His reply was immediate; he even told her he'd take care of the dessert.

It had been a few days since she'd checked her work email. The hotel had hired a contract manager to carry her workload while she took the personal leave to run the Landing, so there wasn't much to monitor until she was ready to return to D.C. She'd been grateful for the company's care and support following her father's death; she hoped their goodwill extended as far as accepting her application for the promotion.

Setting her laptop down on the desk, she opened her email client. One new message from the personnel director waited. Her stomach lurched. Her finger trembled over her laptop's trackpad.

> Dear Ms. Buck,
>
> Firstly, please accept DeVarona International's deepest sympathy for the loss of your father. On behalf of the Luxelle Europe division, I'd like to thank you for your interest in the position of Event Director at Luxelle Santorini. We are impressed with your resume and history of service to the DeVarona hospitality brand, and would be pleased to offer you the position, effective September 30.

Sofia read the rest of the offer with trembling fingers. Her imagination spun out a red carpet of opportunity stretching into the horizon. She could wrap up the season in Hampton; Kevin Landry would find her a buyer for the Landing. Her condo in Columbia Heights would be snapped up in a heartbeat. Judy and Chris could visit and have that honeymoon she'd offered. Visions of white sand, azure skies, and sun-soaked days carried her through the remainder of the day, marred by one persistent question.

How was she going to tell Silas?

Even hours later, when he knocked on her apartment door and let himself in, she still hadn't come up with a perfect answer.

"Hi," she said, closing her laptop to hide her internet search for real estate on Santorini.

"Hey." He crossed the room and leaned over the sofa to kiss her. "How was the rest of your day?"

"Good." She set the laptop on the coffee table, evasions forming on her lips. "Amy and I got some maintenance done on the Old Man; we were busy. You?"

He came around the sofa. "Besides spending a good portion of the day dreaming up ways to get you back into the shower, it was just another day."

"You don't need to work so hard at that, you know." It was so much easier to let him seduce her. "I really ought to shower at least twice a day."

"Yeah?" He crawled over the cushions, leaning in to kiss her neck. "Does that mean we can get dirty first?"

So much easier, she thought, when his body was warm and solid over hers, when she could push his shirt up over his head and lay her hands on the broad expanse of his back.

She gave her mouth up willingly when he kissed her, surrendering to the ease with which their bodies moved together.

Impatient, she reached for his waistband, but he stopped her, kneeling back. Grasping her hips, he tugged her down on the sofa, settling himself between her thighs. Her heart skipped eagerly when he smoothed his palms up over her belly, kneading her breasts gently over her clothes before raising her arms up.

She let them rest behind her on the arm of the sofa

while he unbuttoned her camp shirt and pushed it aside. He watched her, eyes hot with desire, as he parted the fabric, held her eyes while he bared her skin to the cooling evening air. With his mouth he traced the lacy border of her bra as his fingers slipped under the satin. She pushed herself up, half sitting, to shed the shirt and bra.

Silas laid her back and she gave over to him. He took one taut nipple and then the other into his mouth, teasing the sensitive flesh with a delicate scrape of teeth, drawing out the ache of pleasure with his clever fingers.

When her body moved restlessly, pressing against him, he shed the last of his clothing, peeling away her lace and satin, following the fabric with his mouth. She cried out when his tongue teased the center of her wanting. He brought her up slowly, tenderly, taking his cues from her soft sounds, from the skip of her breath. When she tensed against him, he pressed on, pushing her pleasure over the edge.

"Silas." Her hands clutched at his shoulders, drawing him up. "I want you inside me."

He responded to her directness in kind, filling her, gathering her close. They came together with an urgency that shocked her.

They never made it the shower, but woke together before dawn in her bed, bodies tangled. Sofia rolled him under her, taking the lead, bringing them both fully awake with sweetness and heat as the dawn broke over the Atlantic.

SATURDAY WAS WEIGHED DOWN BY A STILL AND sullen heat. Sofia changed her uniform polo twice before

Amy arrived to cover the evening shift. She showered under cold water and dug in her closet until she found a lightweight skirt and tank top. She twisted her hair up off her neck and skipped her face, opting for lip-gloss to finish her outfit.

She went in the main entrance of Atlantis Market. Silas's nephew was restocking the sunscreen display. "Afternoon, Ms. Buck."

At least he didn't call me "ma'am" this time, Sofia thought wryly. "I'm looking for Silas."

"He said you could go on up."

She smiled and headed for the back door and the stairs. Silas met her on the landing in his customary surf shorts and band tee. "Hi, gorgeous."

"Hey," she said, noticing his empty hands. "Where's dessert?"

"We have to pick it up." He touched the tip of her nose. "I didn't forget."

She felt a blush creep over her face. "That's not what I meant."

He kissed her swiftly and jogged down the stairs, opening the door to the store. "Theo! I'm out. You good?"

Theo's muffled reply sounded affirmative, which seemed sufficient for Silas. Sofia marveled at the mysteries of male communication as she followed him out the door.

"Whose ride?" Silas asked.

Sofia jingled her car keys. "Air conditioning."

When they were in the car, she asked him where they were heading. He gave her an address on Route 1. When they arrived, he asked her to pull over so he could run in. Sofia watched him duck into a shop she thought might have once been a diner. The awning over the front door read

"Treat." Candy striped café curtains obscured the interior, but Sofia got the impression of an old-fashioned ice cream parlor.

Silas came out with a reusable grocery bag bearing the Treat logo. He set it in the backseat of her car before sliding in next to her.

Sofia's curiosity got the better of her. "What did you get?"

"Sundae party," Silas replied. "I figured there would be kids, and who doesn't like ice cream?"

JUDY AND CHRIS'S TWO CARS FILLED THEIR SMALL driveway. The house was a Cape Cod cottage with a screened-in breezeway between the house and garage. Both garage bays were open, revealing a lawnmower, snowblower, as well as two bikes, a hefty stroller, and a small aluminum fishing boat. Sofia pulled her car onto the side of the road behind a small SUV. Silas grabbed the bag of dessert and followed her across the front lawn. The smell of hardwood charcoal wafted through the screens from the back.

Her knock on the breezeway door was met with a shout to come through. Judy was perched on the deck railing with an athletic brunette. A man Sofia assumed was Chris Dunaway was manning the grill with Dex Adams. Sofia took the brunette on the deck to be Dex's pediatrician wife.

"Sof!" Judy hopped down and hugged her, squeezing hard. She released Sofia and hugged Silas. "I'm so glad you joined us!"

Silas held up the bag full of sundae fixings for the hostess's inspection.

"Ooh, a Treat Sundae Party?" Judy gave Sofia a significant look. "He can stay."

"Can I put this away?" Silas asked.

"Oh, my lord," Judy gushed. She called over her shoulder to her husband. "Christopher, I'm leaving you for Sofia's boyfriend." Pointing to the breezeway door, she patted Silas's arm. "The kitchen's that way."

Silas took his instructions and left in the direction of the kitchen.

An irritated squawk interrupted their arrival. Judy reached down for an infant carrier parked under the shade of a canvas umbrella, nudging it so it rocked. She rattled a colorful plush ornament hanging in front of the infant buckled inside. "Sof, this is Andie."

Sofia crouched down to run a finger over the baby girl's cheek. "I've heard a lot about you." She looked up at Judy. "She's beautiful. I love that you named her for a Molly Ringwald character."

"*Pretty in Pink*!" Judy squealed. "Laurie, Sofia and I must have watched that movie a hundred times." She pulled Sofia over to the brunette. "Sof, this is Laurie, Dex's wife. Laur, this is my oldest friend, Sofia Buck."

Laurie leaned in for a quick hug. "Dex mentioned he'd seen you in the bar. We knew your father a little. I'm so sorry for your loss."

The other woman's warmth wrapped around Sofia. "Thank you. It's really good to meet you."

Dex called her over to the grill, just as Silas came out from the kitchen to join her. Chris leaned over to kiss her cheek, keeping his tongs and spatula over the grill. "It's a pleasure, Sofia. I've been hearing about you for years."

"I'm sure it was all lies," Sofia laughed.

"Judy tells me you and Decker go way back." Chris greeted Silas with a man-nod. "How's the Jeep?"

Silas shook Dex's hand and looked over the grill full of burgers and bratwurst. "Running great."

"Sof!" Judy called, holding up a pitcher. "Iced tea?"

"If you gentlemen would excuse me," she smiled and headed for Judy and Laurie, who'd moved to deck chairs under the umbrella with the baby.

A burst of childlike laughter heralded the return of the three other children at the party. They came crashing out of the rhododendrons that lined the fence at the edge of the property. The tallest, a tiny version of Chris, raced over to the deck, brandishing a grimy Wiffle ball.

"Dad? Will you play catch?"

Chris shook his head. "Gotta make dinner, Bud."

Two preschoolers trailed behind him, one lean and sturdy, the other still sporting a baby's softly rounded joints. The littlest one looked plaintively at Dex. "Daddy?"

Silas spoke up to the trio of little boys. "Can I play, too? If Dex here isn't scared of my fastball, we've got the makings of a good game."

All three boys lit up. Dex jumped the deck railing to whoops and applause from the kids. "Silas, this little monster," he pointed to the smallest boy, "is my son Henry. The beanpole is Jake Dunaway." He ruffled the older boy's hair. "And his brother John."

Sofia watched Silas choose up teams with Dex and the little boys. She turned to Judy. "You really did name them all for John Hughes characters. I didn't put it together until just now."

Judy grinned. "At least I didn't call Johnny 'Bender.'"

The three women dissolved into laughter. Down in the yard, Silas set himself up as the pitcher and coached Jake and Henry into position. John took up the plastic yellow bat and the game was on. Dex played catcher behind a home plate he fashioned out of a Frisbee in the grass. Silas faked a big wind-up and lobbed an easy pitch at John, who whacked it past Silas's shoulder.

Laurie watched Henry scramble for the ball. "Silas is so sweet with the boys."

Judy looked at Sofia. "Mmhm."

Chris finished with the meat on the grill, and Judy orchestrated the rest of the table setting while she nursed Andie in the shade. The bigger kids managed to sit still long enough to inhale their weight in potato salad and hamburgers before Jake led the charge for dessert.

"Sofia and Silas brought ice cream," Judy informed them. "Go play. We'll call you when it's ready."

Judy, who'd had Andie over her shoulder, got up and deposited the sleeping baby in Sofia's arms. "I have to pee."

For someone so small, little Andie Dunaway was solid and warm in her arms. Sofia scootched in her chair to accommodate the baby and inhaled the powder and milk scent of Andie's peach fuzz hairline.

"So, Sofi," Dex said, freshening everyone's iced tea. "You headed to D.C. when the season's over?"

Sofia felt everyone's focus shift to her. "Yeah," she said, wishing she could dodge the question.

"Judy and I drove by the other night," Chris added. "The Landing looks great. Your old man would be proud."

"Thanks." Sofia picked up her tea with her free hand. Andie didn't stir. She remembered then what Judy had said about Chris and her dad being in recovery together. She gave him the best smile she could muster. "I'm glad you think so."

Silas deflected the line of questioning by asking about

the Dunaway Auto Repair lettering on the back of Jake's baseball shirt. While they discussed the business and rec-league sponsorship, Sofia chewed on her guilt.

Her father wouldn't be proud. He'd be devastated. He'd let his only child go to keep the drink and the pain, but he'd never lost Buck's Landing. She couldn't get rid of it fast enough.

"Sofia? Are you okay?" Laurie was leaning across Judy's empty chair.

"Oh." Sofia set her glass down without drinking from it. "I'm fine. Just woolgathering."

"Do you ever have time off on weekends?" Laurie asked.

"I can, if my assistant manager can come in. Why?"

"Judy keeps forgetting to ask you," Laurie said, casting a maternal eye over the three boys racing around in the yard. "I can't imagine why. She and I are going up to Freeport to do some shopping some time soon, and we wanted to invite you."

"I'd love to," Sofia replied, finding that she meant it. She liked it here on the Dunaways' deck. She liked Dex's wife and Judy's husband, and the kids made everything so cozy —and crazy. Andie stretched slightly, her sleepy weight shifting, and Sofia felt the movement in her heart. She leaned over and kissed the sleeping baby's forehead.

"You want me to take her?" Laurie asked.

Silas interrupted. "Give me the little monkey."

Before Sofia could argue, Silas had transferred Andie to his shoulder, where she nuzzled her face into the hollow between his neck and shoulder, sighing into sleep. Silas caught the wonder in Sofia's expression.

"Theo's got younger siblings. I know how to hold a baby." He was teasing, but Sofia felt an accusation in his tone.

Judy came out with a fresh pitcher of tea and the sundae supplies on a tray. "Brace yourselves." She set the tray on a potting bench she used as a sideboard and hollered. "Ice cream!"

Jake, Johnny, and little Henry flew up the stairs. The stomping woke Andie, who put up a wail. Silas stuck his pinky finger in her mouth and bounced her on his shoulder until she settled.

Chris looked impressed. "You're a pro, Silas. Surprised some woman hasn't scooped you up."

A quick flicker in Silas's expression belied his casual response. "One of these days, one will."

Jake walked over with his ice cream. Chris made room at the table for his son while Judy set out the littler boys' bowls between Laurie and Sofia.

"Jake, did Mommy tell you where Miss Buck lives when she's not running the mini-golf?" Chris asked.

"And the Snack Bar," Jake added solemnly, from around a spoonful of Oreo ice cream piled with whipped cream and fudge sauce. He shook his head as he chewed.

"Washington, D.C.," Chris continued. For the adults, he explained. "Jake's class learned about the nation's capitol last year."

Jake squinted at Sofia. She waited while Judy's son took her measure. "Have you met the President?" Jake asked.

The adults all laughed.

"I have," Sofia replied, very seriously. "At a fundraiser where I work, I got to lead him and his whole security detail down a hallway. At the end of it, I opened a door, and said, 'This way, Mr. President.'"

Jake giggled. "Was he nice?"

"He was, but not as tall as he looks on TV."

"Really?" Judy said. "You really met him?"

"Yeah. I was overseeing a campaign fundraising dinner at the DeVarona."

Judy whistled. "This year you're ushering the Commander-in-Chief. Next year you'll be frolicking on a Greek beach. I think I want your life."

"What's this?" Dex asked. "Sounds promising."

Sofia could feel Silas's stare. She felt her cheeks go red; now wasn't the time. "Oh, nothing," she said lightly. "Just a promotion I applied for."

"Going to be tough to run the Landing next summer if you're in Europe." Chris swiped Johnny's abandoned spoon through the dregs of his sundae. "If you need someone, one of Dex and Laurie's friends is a commercial property manager. She does a lot of that kind of stuff."

Sofia avoided meeting Silas's gaze. "Thanks."

"Speaking of, Laur," Chris went on, "tell Caroline to bring her Acura in if she's still having trouble with her tire pressure sensors."

The conversation turned to people the others knew. Sofia took the opportunity to search out the powder room. When she stood, Judy mouthed directions to her without needing to ask where she was going.

She made it halfway back down the narrow stairs from the second floor when she heard steps approaching.

"Sofia? You okay?"

Silas stood at the bottom of the stairs. He leaned against the wall, the slanting late afternoon sun playing with his hair and the shadows on his face.

She sat down on a stair tread. "Please don't."

"Don't what?" He sat two treads below her.

"Don't say anything about the Landing, about my dad, about Greece or Washington." She pressed her fingers to her temples.

"Okay. I won't." He brushed a hand over her hair. "Are you sure you're okay?"

She breathed deeply. "Yes. I just needed a minute."

Silas stood to leave.

"Silas?"

He stopped at the bottom of the stairs, but didn't turn.

"I was going to tell you."

She held her breath waiting for his reply.

When it came, his voice was soft, almost wistful. "We both have a lot to talk about."

Sofia returned from the bathroom to find baby Andie in her carrier and everyone else engaged in a high stakes game of bean bag toss. Judy and Silas made room for her on their team, along with Johnny and Henry. She played a respectable turn, scoring twice with her four blue bean bags. After three very dramatic innings, however, Jake, Chris, Dex, and Laurie's team was declared the winner.

While they celebrated with high-fives and good-natured taunting, Sofia whispered to her youngest teammates. "They might have won, but you guys picked the best team." Johnny and Henry looked at her with conspiratorial grins. "I always treat my teammates to free mini-golf and ice cream!"

Judy hugged her and high-fived the little boys, who ran to brag to Jake about their consolation prize. Sofia assured Jake that he, too, was welcome to join his brother for a free round. He thanked her with a gap-toothed smile.

SILAS OFFERED TO DRIVE ON THE RIDE HOME, BUT Sofia assured him she was fine.

"You just want to get behind the wheel of a proper car," she teased.

"Well, yeah," he replied. "I'm not stupid."

She gave him a sidelong smile. "Maybe someday."

"Not if you're planning on living a golden expat life in Greece."

He regretted the words the moment he'd spoken them. Her hand tightened on the wheel, white-knuckled.

"Listen," he said quickly, "that's not what I meant."

She stayed silent, focusing on the road, her other hand tense on the gearshift.

"I'm just going to say it," he began. "I had fun tonight. With your friends, with you. I saw you enjoy yourself, too. Just like I saw you enjoy yourself on the strip. You love this town, deep down you do, but you refuse to let yourself trust those feelings because of what happened with your father. I get it, Sofia. I do. I'm not saying it's going to just go away, but if you gave yourself a chance..."

"Then what?" she snapped. "I'll have a good summer? I'll magically be able to put aside everything that drove me away? I'll settle down here? Have some kids; grill some burgers in my backyard?"

She glanced over at him. Her cheeks were flushed, her eyes glittering. For the second time since they'd met, the phrase came to his mind: she was magnificent. While she spoke, he could see it: the house, the kids, the grill, the two of them.

"You might find that staying here is something worth enjoying." He met her anger with cool reason, hoping to take the wind out of her sails. What he got was white-lipped silence for another five minutes.

She pulled the car into her parking space and turned to

face him. "Look, I was going to say something about Greece."

He failed to keep the disappointment out of his voice. "Of course you were."

"It wasn't a sure thing, and I felt weird about it."

It was as if the bottom dropped out of her Beamer. "Wasn't?"

She looked down, her reply scarcely more than a whisper. "They offered me the job."

"How long have you known?"

"Since Thursday." Her eyes were shining when she looked back at him.

He couldn't help the sarcasm. "We spent the night together, Sofia. You didn't consider I might be interested in that news?"

"You don't just casually mention to the guy you're sleeping with that, hey, you're going to move to Greece sometime soon."

Her words punched him in the gut. "So, I'm just the guy you're sleeping with?"

"Silas." She released the wheel, hands twisting in her lap. "I'm sorry."

"Please. Don't apologize." He unbuckled his seatbelt. "I guess I knew that, but you know what? It still hurts to hear."

He caught the slight tremor that shook her lips. He wasn't sure he could take it if she cried again.

"What did you think this was?" Her mouth tightened. He was grateful she held her tears in check. "I was never going to stay here permanently. You knew that."

"I don't know what I thought this was. I do know I care about you. More than I should." He opened the car door, still hoping she'd make some move to keep him there. When she only dropped her gaze to the steering wheel again, he climbed out of her car and walked away. The sound of the slamming door bounced around the parking lot, ricocheting off the adjacent motel walls and the fence that surrounded the Landing.

Ten

Silas's quiet bitterness was fresh in Sofia's mind when her alarm shocked her out of sleep the next morning. She had no memory of leaving her car, no real recollection of coming into her apartment. Even what sleep she'd gotten left no evidence of rest. Her skin was dull, and dark shadows settled below her eyes.

Last night's fight had made up her mind. It was time to leave. Labor Day was a week away; time to close things up and make as clean a break as possible. Sofia choked down a slice of toast with her coffee. She was going to need energy to face everything she needed to get done in the next seven days. Starting with emptying the apartment.

Not knowing fully what to expect, she opened her parents' closet again. This time, she eyed the contents with more than a desire for old vinyl. The memory of Silas's arms and the richness of Dusty Springfield's voice pushed back at her from the shadows, and she fled to the living room for her mp3 player.

Better armed with an upbeat mix of singer-songwriters, she went to work. When she surveyed the damage a few hours later, she gave herself a grudging round of applause. The box of records was stacked with a box of framed photographs and her father's personal effects. His clothing was stacked in a laundry basket to be bagged and taken to the local thrift shop.

She broke for lunch in front her of laptop. The first order of business was emailing HR and formally accepting the offer. The second was calling Judy. Judging from the noise in the background, her kids were home, and perhaps holding the household hostage.

"Sorry," Judy said, pausing to holler at the boys not to wake their sister, "it's a zoo here today. This is twice I'm talking to you in two days. What's up?"

"I got the job."

There was a pause, during which Sofia was certain something was shattered somewhere in Judy's house. When Judy replied, she sounded impressed. "You are getting better at confiding."

"Maybe a little." Sofia braced herself. "I found out three days ago."

Judy only laughed. "Still, at least you're telling me before you disappear."

"I won't be able to make the shopping trip." She hoped her friends wouldn't be too disappointed. "I'm going to have to close the Landing after Labor Day weekend and head back to D.C. I've just got too much to do, and I'm expected in Greece at the end of September."

"So soon?" Judy did sound disappointed, but only for a moment before she muffled the phone and ordered the boys outside to play. "What will you do about the Landing?"

"My real estate agent will keep working on finding a buyer, and didn't Chris or Dex say something about someone who does property management? Maybe I can hire her to keep an eye on the place."

"Caroline, yeah," Judy said. "I'll text you her number later. So, tell me all about Greece."

Judy sighed and swooned over Sofia's description of the Luxelle's amenities and the volcanic beaches, the more relaxed lifestyle and the high class clientele. "You don't suppose I could just leave Christopher here with the kids and find myself some sheik to run away with?"

Sofia dissolved into giggles. "I'm sure I can arrange that."

"If anyone could," Judy trailed off. "I have to ask, where does this leave you with Silas?"

"Nowhere good," Sofia admitted. "We had a terrible fight about it last night."

"Oh, shit. Sorry, hon." The phone was muffled again. "You want to come over for dinner tonight?"

"No, thanks though," Sofia said. "I have to work the register tonight, and I'm trying to get some of the apartment stuff dealt with."

"I want to see you before you leave," Judy warned.

Sofia smiled. "Of course, and I wasn't kidding about the honeymoon trip for you and Chris. I'm going to make it work."

"I never say no to free European vacations," Judy laughed. "That's a personal motto."

Sofia ended the call feeling far better about her future than she had when she'd woken up. Her next call was to Kevin Landry, who assured her that her early departure wouldn't be a problem. He even offered to call Caroline Barclay, with whom he was already acquainted, about looking out for the Landing once it was closed.

With her business settled, Sofia took a long, hard look at

the living room. The furniture was nothing special. There was a pillow and an afghan of her mother's she would keep, and of course the photographs and her mother's milk glass. Nothing she couldn't box up this afternoon.

She couldn't help but linger over the images her father had placed on the mantelpiece. Elena Costa Buck smiled out from a dozen frames, not much older than Sofia was now. Sofia's eyes traced the streak of white hair that had been forming at her mother's temples in one particular close-up. She wondered if, in a few years, she'd be thinking about coloring a similar streak.

Next to the close-up of her mother, a photo of her father pushing her on the old metal swings at the boardwalk playground caught Sofia's eye. Her hair, more unruly then, was blown around her face by the wind, but her joy shone through the dark brown strands. She smiled at the bruised and scraped knees her ten-year-old self hadn't able to avoid.

Her mother had taken the picture while her father pushed her. The image captured the precise moment of contact when he was about to send her forward, high-flying and free. That was what she was supposed to have had, her father behind her, sending her soaring out into the world, fearless and loved. Instead she'd fled in defiance. Instead she'd given up her home to escape.

Was she giving up and running away again? Silas would think so. She could still hear the cold anger in his voice. It certainly didn't help that he was right. He was far more than just someone she was sleeping with. For that, she'd had Elliot.

Elliot would probably love that she was moving to Greece. One more stop on his global jaunts.

The phone rang, startling her out of her reverie. Elliot's name on the caller ID was a shock. She wondered if his ears were ringing. After their unpleasant conversation, she hadn't expected to hear from him so soon.

"Elliot, how are you?" She took the phone back to her bedroom, leaving the photographs and problematic thoughts behind.

———

SILAS STORMED THROUGH THE EARLY PART OF THE day. Theo sensed his mood and laid low, working the register with none of his usual smart-ass banter. Silas's customary ease with shoppers was replaced with stony silence or snarls; the tension in his body held on despite a punishing run in the midday heat. Sofia's secrets and her defiance of the magic between the two of them weighed heavily, as did the way he'd left her, slamming the car door hard enough to feel it under his feet.

She'd started to slip away, to turn on the one foot she'd kept out the door all summer, and like an idiot he'd pushed her through it. He'd seen the bags in the trash cans under her stairs on the way back from his run, seen her hauling more bags to her car. He was a smart enough man to know she was cleaning out the apartment, easing herself away from her temporary life in Hampton.

To hell with that.

"Theo, I'll be back," he barked, and shoved his way out the back door and around the fence.

He kept his steps light on the stairs, not wanting to begin an argument before he even arrived. The door was open, music drifting through the screen. He could see a stack of photos in a cardboard box. Half the mantel was bare, and a bundle of newsprint and packing tape sat on the shelf where Elena Buck's treasures once lived.

"Sofia?" He knocked gently, but got no answer. He tamped down the urge to barge in and demand to have his apology heard, to demand she admit there was more to them than a casual summer fling.

"Sofia?"

"I am sorry." Her voice was faint; he assumed she was back in her room. At first, he thought she was speaking to him, but the playlist on her iPod ended and the truth quickly became apparent in the resulting quiet. "Elliot, you have no idea how wonderful that sounds. I'll be back in Washington in ten days. Let me know when you get back."

He knew that voice, the softness and intimacy of her tone. He knew when he was interrupting. He descended the stairs as quietly as he'd arrived.

SOFIA'S REMAINING WORK DAYS AT THE LANDING took on a new rhythm. She divided her time between her shifts on the course and preparing to leave Hampton, this time truly for good. The apartment was stripped down to the basics she needed to survive. Everything else she'd sent to D.C., care of the DeVarona, until she could arrange for storage and, for some of it, overseas shipping. With the weight of her father's memory divided and packed away, she could almost pretend her heart was whole, but only as long as she kept her gaze from lingering on the Atlantis Market.

Charlotte and Gavin were now rumored to be dating, though they were only flirtatious at the Snack Bar. Amy's erstwhile boyfriend, Jamie, changed his tune and came around one night to see about taking her out after work. August's heat was nurturing love affairs everywhere she looked.

The twenty linear feet between her apartment and Silas's might as well have been the Grand Canyon for all either one of them was willing to cross it.

For the first few days after they'd fought, she'd watched him come in from his morning runs, unwilling to admit missing him was the real reason she was at the window with her morning coffee. After that, she stopped torturing herself. Even so, she felt more attuned to the comings and goings of Silas's Jeep, and Theo seemed to cross her path with unusual frequency.

On the Friday of Labor Day weekend she and Judy had a farewell lunch at The Sandpiper Grill, after which Sofia went up to Portsmouth to meet with Kevin Landry and Caroline Barclay. She did some shopping before driving back, buying a piece of local pottery for her assistant at the DeVarona and a pair of nautilus-shaped cufflinks for the next time she saw Elliot. As a thank you for a summer's hard work, she bought Amy a gift card from Fête. She made a mental note to get small thank you gifts for Charlotte and Gavin, as well.

She was passing a stationery store when she saw the print in the window display.

It was a large ink drawing based on a vintage postcard, tinted with watercolors, showing the Hampton Ballroom and the Bandstand as they'd looked almost a hundred years before. It was perfect for Silas. Assuming he ever painted the apartment or spruced up the old-mannish décor, the print would look beautiful on the wall above where the ratty sofa now sat.

She hesitated, but the urge was so strong that she gave in, buying it and arranging for the shop owner to deliver it to the Atlantis at the beginning of the following week. It was cowardly, she knew, but she couldn't face him, and it seemed obvious he felt similarly. It would be easier for both of them if she just disappeared. Life would go on. She had healed from Hampton's wounds before; she could again, and Silas would find someone new, perhaps even Caroline Barclay.

Once invented, the image of the two of them together took root in her imagination. Try though she might to avoid it through the remaining days of the weekend, her mind conjured up pictures of the curvy brunette accompanying Silas to Dex's bar or the Funarama. When the last of the Labor Day customers left on Monday evening, it was a relief to finally lock the chain-link gate and the steel grate behind the Snack Bar window.

Gavin had hung the panda Silas won for her over the soft-serve machine at some point in the last few weeks. Looking at it in the darkened room, Sofia nearly pulled it down and stashed it in her car for the trip south. Imagining it moldering in a storage locker squeezed her heart; better the panda stay here, where it belonged.

Her employees met her out front to say their farewells. Charlotte and Gavin had pitched in to buy her a Hampton Beach tee shirt, complete with glittery airbrushed lettering, which she promptly tugged on over her tank top.

Amy had commissioned a framed photograph of Buck's Landing from a friend of hers. The goodbyes were bittersweet.

"If you ever come to Europe," Sofia began.

"I promise to find you," Amy finished, hugging Sofia. "Thanks for being a good boss."

"Thanks for being a fabulous manager."

"Are you staying in town tonight?" Amy asked. Sofia saw the younger woman's eyes come to rest on Silas's dark windows.

"No, I have a reservation at my hotel chain's Manhattan property. I'm going to leave now, try to make New York by midnight."

Amy looked at her watch. "You should go, then. Drive safe!"

When her employees were gone, Sofia climbed into the BMW and slipped out of town. She kept the music loud not to stay awake, but to stem the tide of tears that threatened for the first hundred miles.

SILAS CLOSED THE MARKET EARLY ALL THREE evenings of the holiday weekend. Mallory and her husband, Ted, had driven up to move Theo out of his summer apartment, and insisted on treating Silas to nightly dinners. One look at him on arrival and Mallory knew there was something wrong. Come Monday night, she sent her husband and son back to the bed and breakfast at Rocky Bend, and suggested her brother get a beer with her.

"Anywhere but the Salty Cod," Silas said. Mallory raised a questioning brow, but Silas didn't offer her anything further.

In the end, they drove inland to a brew pub in Hampton Falls.

"Silas, I wish you'd told me about this three days ago."

"I need a lecture like a hole in the head, Mal." He picked at the bar napkin under his glass. "I fucked up."

"You did, little brother." Mallory perched on the stool next to him, sandal heels hooked over the rails. "You should have stayed there. A woman hurting is like a wild animal. She snapped at you to protect herself and you abandoned her."

"I abandoned her, Mal? She more or less said she was done with me, that it was just a summer thing."

"And?" Mallory took a sip of her beer.

"And I love her." A few heads turned when he nearly shouted. "I love her, and she's gone, off to a goddamn Greek island with someone named Elliot."

"Elliot?"

"I heard her on the phone." Silas raked back his hair. "I went over there to try to at least apologize, maybe part on friendly terms. I ended up leaving. She never knew I was there."

Mallory sighed. "If you'd told me this on Friday, I would have told you go over there and beg her to stay. On your knees. Warned you that it still might not work." She downed the remainder of her beer and pushed Silas's glass towards him. "Why don't we head back to your apartment? I'll show you the stuff Teddy put together, and we'll get that part settled."

Silas walked his sister up the boardwalk to the Inn at Rocky Bend nearly four hours later. It was well after midnight, and only the stragglers were still awake.

"I'm sorry she broke your heart," Mallory said, looping her arm through his. "Does this mean you'll come home and marry one of my friends? I know an adorable single mom with a little boy in Anthea's class. Very smart girl."

"Not on your life," Silas said.

Mallory laid her head on his shoulder as they walked. "I give up. You really are happier here. This place, it suits you, and I think you're doing the right thing. For the right reasons."

"With a little help from you and Ted."

"Ted's a good man," she said. "I knew it the moment we met."

"So you've said, almost every day since then." Silas took a breath. "I thought I knew about Sofia. I thought maybe she was starting to see that her past didn't need to be her future. I thought she loved me, too."

"Maybe she does, Silas." Mallory reached for his hand, squeezing it affectionately. "It's not always enough."

Silas squeezed back. "I thought if I could just get her to see that her dad wasn't the same monster she remembered..."

"Oh, Silas." Mallory sighed. "You had to know it wasn't that simple."

"I let myself believe it would work out."

"It always has for you, hasn't it?" Mallory spoke without malice, but her words stung nonetheless.

"So, I deserved this?"

"Sometimes hurts run too deep to mend," Mallory said. "I just wish she hadn't wounded you in the process."

They reached the Inn and Silas hugged his sister. "I'll be okay."

"You'll come for Thanksgiving? Mom misses you."

He crossed his heart. "I'll come for Thanksgiving."

He waited until Mallory was safely inside the front door before turning back for the south end of the beach.

The moon was up, just past full, sitting high and cool in the sky. The heat was gone from the night air. The last time he'd walked down the boardwalk in the moonlight, he'd had Sofia by his side, carrying that ridiculous panda. The toasty scent of turning leaves was faint in the air, a whisper of snow under it like a secret. Gone was the heavy breeze, redolent with fryolator oil and cinnamon. The season was changing.

Autumn was coming, and beyond it the long winter. At some point during the summer, he'd begun to hope he wouldn't be spending it alone. Time to turn his energy towards the Market and its upkeep. He had enough put by to spend the winter sprucing the place up, but the Atlantis was no longer his only seasonal asset. There was also the *Elena Sofia* to see to; he needed to make sure she was somewhere safe for the winter.

Visions of her namesake wintering on the shores of the Aegean soured his thoughts of the little sport fisher.

When he got back to his apartment, he packed up the paperwork Mallory had left with him and fell into bed, fully clothed, with Houdini kneading the duvet cover at his side.

Eleven

Sophia dreamed of paper lanterns falling into a glass-calm sea. Each time a lantern touched the surface, it chimed shrilly, the sound wrapping around her ankles as if to draw her into the water. The dream resisted her efforts to reach for the chiming lanterns; wakefulness was sluggish. She disentangled her legs from the twisted sheets and struck blindly out towards her nightstand for her ringing phone. Her fingers closed around it; she squinted at the screen. Nearly ten o'clock in the morning.

She'd arrived at her condo in the early hours of the morning, tumbling into bed exhausted after the drive down from New York. She'd given herself most of the day in Manhattan to catch up with some friends and enjoy the city before returning to Washington, then delayed her departure until well into the evening.

Kevin Landry was on the other end of the call.

"Hi, Sofia. It's Kevin Landry."

She forced her voice to wake up. "Hi, Kevin. What's up?"

"Good news," he said. "I've got an offer."

139

Her first reaction was not the bubble of pleasure she'd expected. A panicky flutter in her stomach rose up through her body, a headache blooming fresh at her temples.

"Is it a good one?"

"Very." Kevin was ready to talk business, she could hear it in his eager tone. "Cash, a group of investors from New Jersey. They're offering your asking price." He paused while Sofia turned the information over in her head. "It would be a very fast process if you accept the offer, and I recommend that you do."

"I need some time to think." She slid her nightstand drawer open, hoping for a bottle of Advil.

"Not too much time," Kevin warned. "This is a fantastic offer, Sofia. I'd hate to see you miss an opportunity to sell. Speaking of which—"

Silently, Sofia likened Kevin's change of topic to a clumsy downshift. Finding a travel sized package of pain relievers, she shook a dose out into her palm.

"I got your email about the change in your situation. Congratulations."

"Thank you." She swallowed three gel-caps dry and shuddered.

"I have a contact in Washington, an agent I've done referral work with before. I'll forward her information."

"That would be great, Kevin. Thanks again."

"You need to move on this offer, Sofia," Kevin warned her gently.

"I know. Now's just not a great time." She sank back into her pillows. "I'll call you in a few hours."

"I hope that's not too late." Kevin's concern was clear in his voice. "I'll speak with you then."

"Wait, Kevin." She clenched her phone hard in her hand. "I'll take it. Go ahead."

"You're doing the right thing." Kevin sounded relieved. "I'll email you the offer for your signature, and you can email or fax it back to me. Either I or a lawyer here in Portsmouth can handle your power of attorney."

Buck's Landing had a buyer, which meant one more thing off her terrifying to-do list. Sofia dropped her phone back onto the bedside table. She sank down and let sleep reclaim her.

WITH THEO GONE AND THE WEATHER TURNING, Silas approached his first week of running the Market in the post-season with a casual attitude. After a run on the beach, he showered and brought Houdini down to keep him company. The cat prowled the aisles and sunned himself in the display windows.

He took a mug of coffee outside midmorning, the better to enjoy the last of the hot days. A pickup truck with Massachusetts tags was parked on the grass in front of the Ebbtide Motel, on the other side from Buck's Landing. He waved at the crew-cut-and-khakis driver, who was unloading tools.

"Morning," the newcomer said, pausing to come shake Silas's hand over the low rock wall that separated the Atlantis from the Ebbtide. "You must be the new guy."

"'Fraid so," Silas said with a smile. The two men exchanged introductions.

His neighbor leaned over, casting an eye over the closed sign on the gate at Buck's Landing. "You see much of Jimmy this summer? Surprised to see the place closed up before Columbus Day."

Silas's heart sank. "I hate to be the one to tell you this. Jimmy passed back in late June."

"Shit." The Ebbtide's owner pocketed his hands. "What's going to happen to it? You know anything?"

Silas sought a diplomatic answer. "Jimmy's daughter ran the place for the summer, but she's selling."

"I used to live over the office here. Was friendly with Jimmy and Elena. Shame what happened to her. How's their little girl? Sofia? Christ, she was a kid the last time I saw her."

"Sofia had a knack for running the Landing." Silas winced at the tight knot of hurt in his chest at the mention of her name. "Too bad she decided not to keep it."

His neighbor shrugged. "Change is the only thing you can count on. Nice to meet you."

Silas watched the other man go. He was about to head inside when another truck pulled up onto the sidewalk in front of the Market.

The window eased down with an electric whir. "Silas Wilde?"

"Yeah," Silas said warily.

The driver killed the engine and hopped out. "Delivery."

Silas took note of the lettering on the door of the truck's cab. It was a stationery and gift store he recalled from visits to Portsmouth. The driver pulled a paper wrapped flat package from the truck bed.

He handed Silas an envelope with the company's letterhead on the flap. "This goes with it."

While Silas leaned the package against the front door of the store, the driver reached back into the truck for an invoice, which he held out to Silas. "Just need a signature."

The truck was gone again as quickly as it had come.

Silas sliced the envelope open with a fingertip. Sofia's handwriting leaped up off the page.

Dear Silas,

I'm no good at goodbyes, and I hate that we fought at the end. I saw this and couldn't help but think of you—of you and me. You love this beach enough for both of us. I hope it's better to you than I was.

Sofia

He tore into the brown paper wrapping, peeling it back to reveal the ink and watercolor rendering of a long-ago Hampton Beach. He crouched down, sitting on his heels to admire the work. He figured from the way the tiny figures populating the picture were dressed, it had to be sometime in the '20s or '30s. The Ballroom and the outdoor bandstand dominated the Boardwalk. The soft colors suggested the haze of heat and high sun. The memory of Sofia and their first evening together on the strip hit him like a fist.

When the tears came, he knelt there on the concrete with the sand scraping his knees and let them fall.

SOFIA ONCE READ THAT IT TOOK THREE WEEKS TO form a habit. As she dressed for the evening's event, a black-tie fundraising dinner for a Senatorial campaign, she figured it had to be true. Three weeks of waking, walking to the gym, sweating through a class, showering and dressing for work, taking the Metro to the DeVarona's Embassy Row location, and coming home to pack up the entire contents of her life certainly constituted a habit, albeit a boring one. She had a week left before her flight to Athens, where she'd be training for another week before moving on to her new position.

At least she was in bikini-ready shape from the fitness classes, she thought, smoothing her hands over the bodice of her rented cerulean satin gown.

With a last check of her hair, she slipped her feet into the fold-away ballet flats she wore to walk in, and tucked the champagne satin sandals she would wear for the party into her tote, along with a clutch she'd picked up at an upscale consignment shop near her condo.

She hiked three blocks and hailed a cab near the Metro station.

Her cabbie had a voice like warm honey, full of musical Caribbean vowels. "Where to, pretty lady?"

"Dupont Circle. The DeVarona."

"You meeting your boyfriend there?" He smiled guilelessly into the rearview mirror.

"No boyfriend. Just work," she snapped, busying herself checking her phone to quash the guilty voice in her head. The taxi driver was only being friendly.

"Somebody out there loves you. I just know it." With that comment, the cabbie turned up the radio and left her to her thoughts. For a moment, back in Hampton, she'd started to believe that. The idea scared her to death. Her throat tightened; she stared out the window as the cab rolled through Adams Morgan. It hadn't been fair to hope Silas would call. She'd made her position clear when she'd left without a proper goodbye, but still, every time she checked her messages she looked for his name.

Fresh tears threatened her carefully applied smoky eyeshadow and mascara. She willed them back, tipped the cabbie well, and entered the building through the staff entrance of the hotel.

Final checks were underway in the ballroom when a low, male voice whispered in her ear. "I missed you."

Her heart leaped into her throat before her brain had a chance to slow her down, she spun on her two hundred dollar heels.

Elliot stood there in his tux and earpiece.

"Elliot."

He pressed a kiss to her temple and whispered in her ear. "Hermit is attending tonight. I assumed you'd have seen the guest list and realized."

His earpiece crackled; he touched her cheek, mouthed "later," and slipped away across the dance floor toward the service entrance. She watched him go, mentally running down the guest list. Elliot's detail was on the manifest, she just hadn't been paying attention. He hadn't specifically mentioned the event to her, but in fairness, the politician's schedule had been known to be somewhat fluid.

She cruised through the evening, putting out fires and running interference such that the movers and shakers attending the event had no idea when things went less than smoothly. Her feet were killing her, but the five thousand dollar a plate fundraising dinner had demanded that the management staff look the part.

Elliot drifted in her peripheral awareness. The slightly salted hair at his temples, his eyes crinkled from perpetual watchfulness, his posture alert and aloof, all of it was as familiar to her as the glittering ballroom and the clammy air outside. All of it forced a comparison with the baking heat and sea breezes in Hampton, with Silas's sun-streaked hair and easy smile. She pushed him out of her thoughts and slipped out of the ballroom, ducking outside to the alley where the staff smoked on their breaks.

A young man she didn't know wearing chef's whites

and the cap of a line cook was finishing up a cigarette and a Coke. "Five grand a pop wasn't fancy enough for you, sweetheart?"

Sofia flashed her DeVarona staff card. "Would you speak to your boss like that?"

The cook scowled, the back of his neck reddened as he dropped his cigarette butt and stamped it out.

A pair of tuxedoed men came around the shadowed corner of the building. Sofia knew from their posture and demeanor that they were part of Hermit's detail. As they came into the light, she realized one was Elliot.

Elliot wasn't what he was without reason. He sensed the tension as he approached. "Everything okay here, Ms. Buck?"

She quashed the giggle that bubbled up. Of course he would retain his professional facade in front of a perceived threat. "I'm fine, Agent Winter. Thank you."

Elliot's companion glanced at the still smoldering filter on the asphalt. "You'll want to pick that up, son."

She watched the two agents vanish into the shadows and walked back inside without a word to the young man, who was bent over to retrieve his cigarette.

Elliot found her one last time that evening.

She was changing back into her ballet flats, considering an offer to go out for an impromptu goodbye drink with some of her waitstaff, when Elliot entered the room.

There had been a time when his commanding presence and classic good looks had charmed her. Now, despite herself, she yearned for Silas's less demanding self-possession, the way he slipped into a room. The way he had slipped into her heart, into the fabric of her life.

"Can I come by later?" Elliot asked.

Sofia shot a look at the group of servers waiting on her

near the staff entrance. "I can't, Elliot. I've got plans with the event staff tonight. Another time?"

In a rare show of public affection, Elliot circled her waist and drew her in. His lips cruised knowingly over hers before he whispered low in her ear. "Or maybe in Greece?"

He was gone without another word.

Her colleagues clapped and whistled the second the door closed.

"Well done, hot stuff," one of the bartenders laughed.

She forced a laugh, but her lips were cool, her heart unmoved.

WHEN JUDY DUNAWAY CALLED, SILAS contemplated not answering his phone. The last thing he needed was another reminder of Sofia.

"Silas, it's Judy. I need a favor."

He already knew he would end up saying yes. "What's up?" he asked.

"Jake's soccer team needs a second coach. Please tell me you know how to play."

"I played some," he said hesitantly. He could remember countless autumn Saturdays spent playing in one youth soccer league or another, feeling frosty morning air in his lungs and the damp green field under his cleats.

"Christopher signed up to coach with another of the dads, but the other guy dropped out two weeks into the season. I told Christopher I'd make a few calls, since he's at work all day today. I'm only calling you. Dex has three left feet, and I saw how good you were with the boys."

"How soon do you need someone?" The truth was, he couldn't think of any reason not to do it.

Judy's reply was a little sheepish. "Tomorrow morning for a team meeting."

"I'm only doing it for you," he teased.

"Liar," she laughed. "You don't have anything else going on. Not since..." She stopped cold. "Not since the tourist season ended."

Silas heard the sentence she didn't finish. Not since Sofia left. "Where should I be tomorrow, and when?"

"I'm sorry. I swear to god, three pregnancies destroyed my ability to think before I speak. I'll have Christopher text you about the meeting."

He felt bad. He liked the Dunaways, and he didn't want them to feel like they couldn't speak to him about Sofia. After all, she'd left Judy behind, too. "No worries, Judy. Have you heard from her at all?"

"Nope. Not since Labor Day." There was a pause; Silas could hear children in the background. "I saw her before she left. She told me you two fought. She didn't want to talk about it, and it's probably not my place to say anything, but I think she made a mistake, and I think somewhere under all that armor, she knows it."

"Yeah, maybe," Silas replied. He didn't know what to say. "Anyway, have Chris shoot me the details, and I'll see him tomorrow."

"Thanks, Silas."

He set his phone down on top of the stack of paperwork that had arrived that morning, wondering how the Dunaways would feel about what those documents represented. He hoped that when Judy inevitably told Sofia, she'd understand.

And forgive him.

Twelve

ith the movers due in just a few hours to take what was left of her things to a long-term storage facility, Sophia finally turned her attention to the two boxes she'd been avoiding. One, a cardboard box she'd pulled out of the back of their closet back in Hampton bearing her mother's name in her father's expressive handwriting. The other, a hastily packed box of mementos from the summer. She hadn't yet forced herself to open either. Instead, they'd taunted her from a corner of her living room as the days remaining in her condo dwindled.

Kevin Landry's referral had taken her to a sleek but comfortable real estate agency in Georgetown. She'd listed the condo the same day; it had shown twice in the first forty-eight hours. She'd taken the first reasonable offer, after less than a week on the market. That closing would happen after her departure.

The sale of Buck's Landing had gone without a hitch, with the attorney in Portsmouth signing the paperwork for her. By the time she finished her orientation week in Athens and moved on to Santorini, there would be nothing left to tether her to her old life.

Feeling like a coward, she opened the second box—the one she'd packed herself—and parted the crumpled newspaper protecting the contents. Inside, the purple glass mermaid preened on her purple glass rock. Beside her rested the beachy lobster in his preposterous shorts. Her words that day at the snack bar window had come true. The mermaid was off to see the world. Sofia suppressed a pang of envy; the glass statue had a companion for her travels. She gathered up the mermaid and the lobster, and carried them back to her bedroom where her large suitcase waited, along with several boxes of personal effects and clothing she was shipping to herself care of Luxelle.

She added the *tchotchkes* to a box already holding her favorite of her mother's vases and the pile of photos from the Hampton apartment. Those she would take with her.

The final box's dusty, dented corners suggested its contents hadn't seen daylight in some time. Inside was her mother's wedding dress. It had been a simple affair, made by Nonna from her own dress's silk and lace. The cloth was yellowed and smelled of long-staled mothballs, but Sofia could still see how beautiful the dress had been. The memory of poring over her parents' wedding photos swamped her.

She noticed an envelope, standard letter-sized and far newer than the wedding dress, tucked carefully into the bodice of the gown. Hands trembling with emotion, she reached for it. Again, her father's bold letters spelled out her mother's name. It was thick; there were too many pages inside to have fit easily. Feeling like an eavesdropper despite her curiosity, she swiped her stinging eyes on her sleeve and tore the envelope open.

Elena, my love,

It's more than fifteen years since you left me and I still wake up in the morning and look for your hair curling over the pillowcase. If heaven is the boot heel of Italy like your Mama always said, I bet you two have one hell of a garden growing. I was never much good at that, nurturing things, not without you. I miss you. I've missed you every day. Even the really bad ones.

So much that I lost myself, forgot to keep living, forgot to care for our beautiful daughter.

God, Ellie, I screwed up. I drank away my sorrow and I left her on her own. By the time I pulled myself together she was gone, so far so fast and I couldn't ask her to come back. I screwed up so bad. I've been sober now for a while, and I'm supposed to atone, to make my apologies to the people I hurt, but it seems selfish to find her just to unburden my heart. I won't hurt Sofia. I won't dredge up all that pain just to polish up my halo. Instead, I'm saying I'm sorry the best I can to you.

I'm sorry.

I think about her all the time, Ellie. I think she's older now than you were when we got married. She always looked like you. I bet she's a beautiful woman, just like her Mom. I guess she could be married, could even have kids of her own by now. Thing is, sometimes I get angry, so angry at her for leaving me, too. But I drove her away and that's different, and I forgive her for leaving.

I still love both my girls so much.

If I could, I'd tell our daughter to love hard, to give herself up to loving someone. Then I'd tell her to fight hard for it, not to let it walk away, not to let it die, not to let anyone or anything stand between her and real love, even if it hurts like hell, because living without love isn't living at all. I had you. I had that love and maybe I couldn't win against death, but I didn't fight the demons that got between me and Sofia. I let her down, I let me down, and I've got half a life wasted to show for it.

Forgive me, sweetheart, and maybe someday we'll all get another shot.

Love you forever.

Jimmy

Long ago dried tears spattered the ballpoint ink, bled out the pale blue lines of her father's notebook paper. Sofia paged through the stack of letters, all from her father to her mother, all written in the years he was sober. After the first one they became more like journal entries, full of the language of love and loss in a way Sofia had never imagined her father to think.

She lost track of how long she sat there, getting to know the man her father had become. She basked in his forgiveness, finally able to see his remorse, to believe he'd loved her despite his actions. When the letters were read, she folded the pages back into their envelope. Setting it aside, she boxed up the dress. Before she left, she would take it to the cleaners and see about having it preserved, and stored.

A knock at the door pulled her thoughts back to the present. The moving truck waited, pulled halfway up on the sidewalk outside. Dazed, she showed them the furniture and boxes destined for her storage unit. When they had gone, leaving her with a mattress to sleep on and the few things she planned to take to the Salvation Army before she left at the end of the week, she drifted through her rooms. Pared down to the essentials, she didn't amount to much.

The letters called to her from the spot on the kitchen

counter where she'd left them. *I'd tell her to fight hard for it, not to let it walk away, not to let it die, not to let anyone or anything stand between her and real love, even if it hurts like hell, because living without love isn't living at all.*

She was moving towards the bedroom, grabbing her carefully packed suitcases before her head could stop her. She raced down the front steps and around the corner to the alley where her car was parked, dragging her luggage behind her. She was outside the Beltway and halfway to Baltimore before she allowed herself to think.

The Landing was gone; her condo was gone. Luxelle was expecting her in eight days. Silas had never said he loved her. Not in words. She'd never said she loved him, but she did. Her foot nudged the accelerator, pushing the speed limit as far as she dared. Even if he turned her away, she owed it to them both to tell him the truth.

HAMPTON BEACH WAS SHROUDED IN DARKNESS when she pulled up outside Buck's Landing. Sofia was quivering from exhaustion, her eyes burning from a punishing, nearly ten hour drive. She'd stopped only once for fast food, gas, and a bathroom, determined to find Silas before she lost her nerve altogether.

She opened a window and let the BMW idle. The ocean was a constant, even in the small hours of the night. The sand was bone-white under a sliver of moon, and Buck's Landing hulked, empty and closed-off, over the mini-golf course. The Landing was dark, but a light glowed in Silas's apartment over the Atlantis Market. Her folly washed over her. For all she knew, he had a woman up there, or he didn't even live there anymore. Three weeks was long enough for anything to have happened.

Steeling herself, she killed the engine and opened the car door. Ocean Boulevard was deserted, save for the streetlights. Her eyes traced the chain-link fence that surrounded the putting greens, coasting over the Snack Bar window, and coming to rest on the unlocked and open gate. Her heart kicked over. What the hell?

She walked in the moonlit shadows towards the gate. Without the cheery burble of the water feature and the piped in top forty, a sinister pall fell over the landmarks. As she rounded the building onto the first green, she heard a voice.

"Goddamn it!" Footsteps on the gravel. "Get the hell over here."

Sofia pulled her phone out of her pocket, fingers poised over the screen.

"Jesus, we've been through this. Not at night when everything's all locked up." The voice was hoarse, urgent in the darkness.

She peered around the man-made cave that separated the front nine from the back nine and nearly laughed in relief. By the light of an LED flashlight, Silas was staring up at a furry face with reflective eyes peering down from the top of the Easter Island Head on the seventeenth hole.

She couldn't help herself. "Lost your cat?"

Silas whipped around, his face a fright-mask in the bleached-out light.

Houdini chirped and skittered down the statue, leaping from the moai's nose and coming to rest at Sofia's feet. Silas watched warily.

"Sofia?"

She scooped up the cat, whose entire body was vibrating with feline joy. "Hi."

Silas pocketed his hands. "Hey. You're a long way from home."

"Am I?" She ran her hands through Houdini's silky fur. The question hung weightily in the air.

"Isn't home about to be the volcanic shores of the Greek Isle of Thera?" Silas winced at his own sharpness.

"Right now?" Sofia's voice broke. "Home feels like an apartment over a mini-golf course."

For a long moment Silas said nothing, his face impassive in the glow of the flashlight.

"Thank you for the print," he said finally. "It was a wonderful goodbye gift. I didn't deserve it."

"You're welcome." Sofia set the cat down. Houdini sat back on his haunches and groomed his tail enthusiastically. "I've been an idiot."

"How so?"

Sofia hoped she wasn't imagining an echoing longing in his reply.

Her words were barely more than a whisper; her heart was beating so hard she could feel it in her fingertips. "I spent so much time and energy running from my father's ghost that I was blinded to the fact that I was repeating his mistakes. I let someone I love slip away, and I was too proud to fight to get him back."

She saw a tiny flicker, a muscle working in his jaw. Her every cell was tuned to his reaction.

"I love you, Silas. I love you, and I'm sorry." Someday, she thought, I will run out of tears. "I know there isn't a place for me here anymore, but I couldn't leave without you knowing you were right. You were so much more to me, and I was frightened and angry and—"

"Shh." His arms came around her, his breath warm on her cheek. "Shh."

He took her face in his hands, drying her tears with his thumbs. "I love you, Sofia. And if we love each other, there's a place for you here."

His mouth was warm when he kissed her. She held him, lips hungry against his. Her hands smoothed up his back, gliding over the smooth skin and muscles she remembered so well. Houdini twined through their legs, breaking the moment.

Sofia looked around at the deserted golf course. "We should go, shouldn't we? We are trespassing."

———

THEY WEREN'T TRESPASSING, BUT HOW TO explain that to her?

"Yeah," Silas began, but Houdini streaked off out the gate and they gave up conversation to follow him. Silas threaded his fingers with hers, loathe to let her go even to walk to the apartment. The cat led the way past Sofia's car, rubbing his back along the doors and tires as he passed.

"I need to move that into the parking lot," Sofia said, voice jittery with adrenaline.

"Leave it for a minute. It's okay," Silas said, pulling her close again, "I don't want to let you go just yet."

He buried his nose in her hair, kissing his way down her neck, tasting the thin skin over her collarbone, hands roaming every inch he could reach. She was real, inexplicably there; his heart was full to the brim.

She touched his face softly, tentatively. "Silas? I know I've made a mess of things; there's so much we need to talk about."

He shushed her with a kiss. "There's something I need to show you. Leave the car and come upstairs."

He took her hand again, squeezing a little in reassurance, and clicked his tongue to call the cat. "Houdini!"

The cat vaulted up the back stairs, rubbing his jaw against the door jamb. Silas opened the apartment door, watching Sofia's eyes move over the room. She took in the changes and looked up at him with eyes full of questions.

"You have my father's chair."

He reached for a curling lock of hair in her ponytail. "It was being loaded onto a Salvation Army truck. You have to admit, it's better looking than the tweedy monster that was here before."

A grin twitched at the corner of her mouth. He leaned over to press a kiss there. She turned to him, capturing his lips with hers, drawing away with a smile and a glance at the print on the wall.

"That's exactly where I imagined it."

"You're exactly where I imagined you," he countered.

Sofia looked out the window that faced the darkened sign at the Landing. "That's good, because right now I don't have anywhere else to go."

"That's what I wanted to show you." Silas pulled open the drawer underneath the patch of kitchen counter where he kept his laptop and pulled out an envelope full of papers. "You'll always have somewhere. If you want it."

He slid the envelope across the counter.

He watched realization and disbelief dawn on her face as she read. She blinked, half-smiling. "You?"

"I couldn't bear to toss that poor abandoned stuffed panda out on the street." He crossed to her, holding her hands over the paperwork. "It's all yours if you want it back."

THE CONTRACTS WERE READY TO BE SIGNED, turning the business and the property back to her. He'd saved it. Arrogant, high-handed, marvelous man.

Sofia grabbed the pen that lay near the drawer. Hastily she scrawled a line of text, then two long slashes. She signed the contract and initialed her changes before handing everything back to him.

She watched him read, watched his face light up.

"This is really what you want?" he asked. "A full partnership? You and me?"

"No," she said quickly. "No. I want a lot more than that. I want the apartment to be a home again, full of laughter and my mother's recipes. I want to save you from brown laminate counters and an old man's cast off sofa. I want you to take me fishing on my father's boat." She cast an eye at Houdini, who sprawled on the battered leather chair. "I even want your damned cat."

She took the contracts and tossed them on the coffee table. "I want a life with you. In Hampton. A full partnership and all that comes after."

Silas's eyes filled. He blinked to clear them, but his voice was hoarse. "You even want my cat." He touched his lips to her hand, to her forehead, and finally her mouth. "I love you."

She glanced at the print she'd given him, thought of her own place in Hampton Beach's long history and just how close she had come to losing it, how close she'd come to walking away from Silas. She brought her gaze to rest on Silas's face, on the answering shine in his eyes.

"I love you, too."

Want an exclusive peek into Sofia and Silas's future?
https://bit.ly/SofiaSilas

Also by Cameron D. Garriepy

THORNTON VERMONT

Damselfly Inn

Sweet Pease

Family Practice

Sugaring Season: Stories from Thornton & Beyond

Bread & Promises (Yuletide)

The Best Laid Plans: A Socially Distanced Thornton Vermont
Romance

Tempests and Temptations: Two Christmas Romances

GREEN MOUNTAIN HEARTS

Ambitious Heart

Unbound Heart

Troubadour Heart

STANDALONE ROMANCE

Buck's Landing

MORE CHRISTMAS MINI-ROMANCES

Cinnamon Girl (Wish)

The Soloist (Joy)

About the Author

Cameron D. Garriepy attended a small Vermont college in a town very like Thornton. She's missed it since the day she packed up her Subaru and drove off into the real world. Some might say she created the fictional village as wish fulfillment, and they would be correct.

She is the author of the Thornton Vermont series, and the founder of Bannerwing Books, a co-op of independent authors. Prior to Bannerwing, Cameron was an editor at Write on Edge, where she curated three volumes of the online writing group's literary anthology, Precipice. Cameron appeared in the inaugural cast of Listen to Your Mother – Boston, and irregularly contributed flash fiction to the Word Count Podcast.

Since her time at Middlebury College, Cameron has worked as a camp counselor, nanny, pastry cook, an event ticket resale specialist, and an office manager. Cameron's ghost-writing and editing hides in the tech and finance sectors. In her spare time, she is an archer, a baker, a gardener, a knitter, and a reader of a lot of romance novels.

Cameron writes from the greater Boston area, where she lives with her husband, son, a very silly pug, and four naughty hens.

Connect with Cameron online at
www.camerondgarriepy.com

Hear first about sales and new releases via Cameron's
newsletter—subscribe at
bit.ly/smartsexynewsletter
Join the conversation in Cameron's Facebook group at
bit.ly/thorntonfbgroup

amazon.com/author/camerondgarriepy

facebook.com/camerondgarriepy

twitter.com/camerongarriepy

goodreads.com/camerondgarriepy

bookbub.com/authors/cameron-d-garriepy

instagram.com/camerongarriepy

pinterest.com/camerongarriepy

Excerpts

Check in to the *Damselfly Inn* and fall in love with Thornton, Vermont:

Over the southwestern end of Lake Champlain, on the New York side, the storm was stirring up the lake water, whipping itself into a frenzied spiral between the high wall of the Adirondacks in New York and the rolling Green Mountains of Vermont. Electricity flashed and crackled between the clouds, dancing down over the water, licking at the shoreline as the storm approached.

Thunderheads cast the Adirondack Suite into shadow. Nan Grady closed the windows and took a long look at the room around her. When the storm hit, at least the jewel of the Damselfly Inn's six guest rooms would stay dry.

A low roll of thunder growled. Nan trailed her hand along the natural cherry-wood sleigh bed as she passed, caught her reflection in the repainted Victorian mirror in the en suite bathroom. She let out a breath of self-approval; everything was exactly as she'd imagined it. Admiring the freesias she'd arranged in a milk glass vase, she straightened the hand-embroidered dresser scarf she'd bought at a church bazaar the weekend after she'd closed on the house.

The third story of the house was smaller than the two main levels, and there was already a full bathroom tucked into the gable. Nan had known the first time she'd seen the house that it would take minimal effort to transform the two small rooms into a bedroom and sitting room.

She'd poured her heart into the third floor, creating a haven for fairytale romance. Splurging on satiny cotton linens for the bed and oversized, lush towels in the bath, searching antique shops and flea markets for the chaise and love seat in the sitting room, spinning her dreams of romance and luxury and her inherent practicality into a snug retreat.

Her Gran had always told her she had an old soul. She supposed it must be true. At 31, her most devoted relationship was with a century old house.

In the deepening shadows, she imagined newlyweds at the window, flushed with joy and anticipation. She could almost hear the sigh of the bride as the man she loved loosened the stays on her gown, the two of them bathed in the rose light of a late summer Vermont sunset.

She closed and locked the suite's door, stopping to rub a smudge on the door's pewter nameplate with her sleeve. The fragrance of the freesias followed her as she headed downstairs.

Downstairs, she tidied up her office and took the opportunity to go over the instructions delivered with the next day's pastries. She'd need to put the tray of croissant and Danish in the fridge in the morning, so they could defrost throughout the day, before going into the warming tray overnight to proof. Her best friend—and pastry chef—insisted that a slow final rise was essential if she wanted the pastries to be perfect for Sunday breakfast.

Nan had to laugh. She and Kate had studied the basics of pastry together, put in the same early hours at the school's patisserie together, but Kate wasn't likely to leave anything to chance when it concerned her finished product.

The darkening clouds blotted out the setting sun. The storm was looking like a sure thing. She decided to batten down the hatches and retreat upstairs to her private apartment over the garage. She could make phone calls and check e-mail from the comfort of her snug sitting room.

While the storm grew in intensity and barreled across the lake and valley, Nan gathered up her laptop and phone, closed and locked the door to her office. On the way through, she snagged the day's mail from where she'd dropped it on the kitchen table earlier and headed upstairs.

With visions of a busy inn dancing in her head, she sorted through the pile of catalogs and bills, dropping the junk mail into a recycling pile on the floor. The postcard stood out from the rest of the post, with its too-bright, beachy vista and a bikini-clad model on a towel splashed across it. She turned it over, scanning the back. It was addressed to a Danny Beaudette. Nan couldn't help reading the broad, looping penmanship on the back. Hey Danny, miss you. The beach doesn't really look like this at all. It kinda sucks. Wish you could come visit. Ellie.

Nan set the card with the bills, making a mental note as the storm threw itself down on the farmland to drop it at the post office on Monday. There weren't any Beaudettes in the neighborhood, but the postmaster was likely to know who the card was meant for. The storm blew into the valley, kicking against the trees and homes like an angry child. The wind howled and rain railed against the windows. Whoever Danny was, Nan hoped he got to visit Ellie at the beach someday.

She smiled to herself as she opened her bookkeeping software, determined to stay focused on the inn. Her spirits flagged a little at the low numbers in the black columns. She wasn't in serious debt, but she would need every reservation she could get to keep it that way, between the mortgage and the business loan.

The local bank had taken a chance on her, and loaned her the start up money in addition to her mortgage. She'd been lucky to have a nest-egg large enough to make the down payment and cushion the loan, and she knew it.

She looked at the collection of photographs on her painted pine bookshelf. Her grandfather had built it for her when she was born, and now his careworn face and that of her grandmother graced its shelves.

Her grandparents had been frugal New Englanders, living a productive and restrained life. Growing up with them, Nan had never wanted for the necessities, but her Gran and Grandpa had never felt the need for extravagances. They had been stern, but loving, and when they had passed away, Nan found they had left her with enough to put a down payment on this house, on her dream.

Despite the personal sacrifices she knew were ahead, she was certain she could make the inn a success. For her grandparents.

For herself.

The storm continued its tantrum as it drove eastward, rushing up to and over the Green Mountains like water over a spillway. Rain pelted down, blown nearly horizontal, and the huge maple tree behind the inn groaned in protest.

Nan was pulled out of her thoughts by a vivid flash of lightening. A sickening crack echoed against the back of the house; a crash shook the whole house, followed by a growl of thunder.

Nan sat frozen for a heartbeat, then she was on her feet and running down from her apartment, through the kitchen and into the foyer. She scrambled into her office and grabbed a hefty flashlight. A cold wind tumbled down from the third floor.

With a hard knot of dread already forming in her stomach, she raced up to the third floor landing. She yanked open the door to the Adirondack Suite with her heart pounding.

She cried out as if she'd been struck. Rain was pouring in through the remains of the gabled roof, lumber and insulation hanging down like broken bones and torn flesh. The hot smell of ozone was fresh in the air. Shingles and debris littered the floor. The silk drapes whipped and snapped at the sills. A limb from the ancient maple tree that grew next to the house lay across the sleigh bed, its raw end sizzling.

"Oh, god. No," she said aloud to the empty room, her voice swallowed by the noise of the storm. "No."

She forced herself to loosen the death grip in which she held the doorknob. She forced herself to inhale and exhale. If she let herself cry now, she would fall to pieces. She jumped when a man's voice called her name from downstairs.

"Miss Grady? Hello! Is anyone up there? Hello?"

She thought of her phone, waiting for her back in her apartment. The man calling knew her name, but she had no idea who she was facing, alone in the house in a storm. She gripped the flashlight tightly and started slowly down the stairs.

They all reached the second story landing at the same time. Nan stopped short in relief. Walt Fuller, the dairy farmer from down the road, stood in the second floor hallway in a dripping slicker and muddy boots, with a similarly dressed younger man at his side.

"Miss Grady? Are you all right?" Walt asked, catching his breath.

Nan almost laughed at the absurdity of the question. She was far from all right. There was a tree branch in her bridal suite. There were muddy boot tracks on the hallway runner. She could feel panic welling up again. Then she saw Walt's expression, and realized they must have heard the lightning strike, seen her roof, and come running to find out if she'd been underneath it.

She was all right. The suite was another story.

"I'm fine, Mr. Fuller. The room upstairs—" she began.

She started to shake and pressed her hand against her mouth, fearing she might be having hysterics.

"Come on down to the kitchen, now, Miss Grady. Molly's making tea for you, and Joss here's going to go take a look at your damage," said Walt, gesturing to his companion.

As Walt Fuller put a hand on her shoulder and steered her towards the stairs, she looked back at the younger man. He gave off an impression of quiet competence that momentarily quelled the panic brewing in her belly, and his eyes were the same shade as the thunderheads outside.

In the kitchen, Molly Fuller was boiling water and getting out the tea and teapot.

"I went ahead and poked around your kitchen, hon. I

hope that's ok," she said to Nan, before turning to her eyes to her husband. "How bad is it?"

"Joss'll tell us in a minute. I sent him on up," Walt replied. He joined his wife at the counter.

"Mr. and Mrs. Fuller, thank you—" Nan started.

"None of that, now," Molly interrupted. "We've barged into your house; we're past formalities. I'm Molly, he's Walt, and we're all neighbors. We take care of our own. Now, I put a fair amount of sugar in this one. It'll help with the shock." She handed Nan a mug.

The mug was solid and warm, the tea sweet and strong. She felt the panic begin to dissipate, the knot of dread loosen. She took a deep breath, and remembered her manners.

"I hope you'll call me Nan, then," she said to the two of them. She almost blushed to note that Walt was holding his wife's hand. "There are cookies from Sweet Pease on a plate under that pie dome, if you'd like."

Molly smiled, "Your mother raised you well."

"My Gran, actually," Nan found herself smiling in response. "My grandparents raised me. My mother passed away when I was small, and my father was never what you could call present." She flushed, feeling she'd revealed too much to these kind people. "Joss...is your son?" she asked, hoping to shift the topic of conversation away from her rootless past.

"He is," answered Molly. "Joss is short for Josiah. Contractor and carpenter, so you're in good hands. He'll get things buttoned up for you tonight, and I'm sure he'll come back in the morning to do a proper estimate, if you'd like."

The man himself walked into the kitchen, wiping a hand on his jeans; he carried his slicker in the other. Rain clung to his hair, leaving damp streaks on his shirt as it beaded and rolled off. His presence filled the kitchen.

"Mom, my ears are burning," he said, a smile in his voice.

Something like envy kindled in her heart. The Fullers had that intangible ease that came with love and familiarity. They were family.

Molly introduced them, "Josiah, this is Nan Grady. Nan, our son, Josiah Fuller."

"A pleasure, Nan, circumstances notwithstanding," he said, reaching for her hand. "And please," he said with a wry look at his mother, "Call me Joss."

"I will. It's nice to meet you, too." Or it would be, she thought, if my livelihood wasn't in serious trouble.

She put her hand in his. Their eyes met over the handshake. A current flared between them. She was sure she must be blushing. His hands were calloused, warm, pleasantly rough. She wondered how they would feel sliding up her back, running through her hair.

"Well, son, what needs to be done tonight?" Walt asked, interrupting her wayward thoughts. She almost laughed; she was more in shock than she'd realized.

Nan pulled her hand away, but she wasn't sure what to do with it. It took her a moment to realize that Joss was speaking to her.

"Miss Grady, have you got tarps and rope? Tie-downs? I'm going to get up on the roof and cover the hole until morning. The rain's clearing off, but I don't want to leave that hole exposed. You're lucky." He said. "There's no wiring or plumbing in that section of ceiling."

Maybe she'd imagined the heat, the spark between them. Joss didn't seem affected by it at all. Maybe it had been so long since she'd looked up from her goals that the first good looking man she'd seen had set her skin humming.

"I've got some tie-downs in my car, but no tarps," she said, wishing she'd thought to buy them on one of her many trips up to Burlington for supplies.

"That's no trouble at all," he replied, turning away from her. "But Dad, I'll need to borrow some from you, and come back."

"I'll help you get some from the barn," Walt said. "Let's not keep the poor girl up all night."

"I think I'll be up anyway," Nan sighed.

"Nonsense, Nan," Molly said. "I'll stay to help you clean up."

Flustered by her neighbors generosity, Nan started to tidy the tea tin and sugar bowl.

"Please, Molly, Walt," she turned to them, embarrassed but resolute, "I can handle it tonight."

Molly met her eyes before getting up and clearing the mugs. Nan hoped the older woman understood what she saw there. She needed to fall apart and pull herself back together again in peace.

Molly rinsed out the tea pot, and dried her hands. She took a key from her pocket and set it on the island. "I can be over first thing in the morning, if you like, and you're going to want to put that key back under the mat," she said with a wink.

Nan stared at the key as Molly bustled out the kitchen door, followed by her men. In all the panic and confusion, she hadn't given a thought to how the Fullers had gotten into the house. She was grateful Molly Fuller had figured out where her spare key was; she supposed it wasn't a very original hiding place.

"Molly, wait!" she called. "Take the key. If I ever need it, I'll know where to look."

Joss, who'd been the last to go through the kitchen door, turned and took the key from her outstretched hand.

Keep reading at https://books2read.com/DamselflyInn

They didn't mean to fall in love during a global pandemic, but misfortune can only delay the best laid plans...

"I know, I know," Poppy said to Mathilda, the plump Golden Laced Wyandotte hen who liked belly rubs and was occupying the picnic table near the run, "I'm wearing mascara. But it's because I like it, not because that woman thought I was the housekeeper."

Mathilda regarded her with aviary nonchalance before hopping down to scratch at an ants' nest she found in the grass.

The sun was out and the breeze was blowing fluffy clouds across the sky, so Poppy was free ranging with the chickens while she worked. The picnic table caught the last vestiges of the household internet connection, allowing Poppy to bring her laptop out and monitor Professor Bixby's classes.

The mascara was a whole lot of too little too late, but she did enjoy the effect. The thin veneer of professionalism she'd cultivated working for Thornton College's History Department had entirely faded since the lockdown started. She favored unstructured skirts with pockets and stretchy tees and tanks in her free time. Her freshly washed curls would look decidedly untamed after air drying without any product, but it didn't really matter. The chickens didn't care, her laptop's camera–like the mic––was off.

With the exception of snooty Elisha, Poppy hadn't seen anyone but the cashier at the Thornton Co-op in days.

Professor Bixby finished his video lecture, and Poppy watched as the individual tiles of his forty-two students closed. She emailed the attendance list, a summary of the lecture, and a transcript of the student questions from the chat to the professor's inbox. *If only he would learn to look at some of those things for himself...*

She was closing her computer when a lost Hemsworth wandered out of the woods.

Or, upon closer inspection, a previously undiscovered, Forty-Something Hemsworth? At least six rangy feet, soulful eyes and a generous mouth, with a twig in his hair, just where a few silver strands shot through the rich brown.

The laptop nearly slipped as Poppy shot to her feet, heart hammering.

"Oh, hey. Sorry," he said, coming to a stop as The Orpington Twins, Lavender and Buffy, flapped over to him. *Shameless hussies.* Forty-Something Hemsworth took in the ever-so-charming coop and run, the profusion of lilacs, even Poppy herself in a swift, unnerving gaze. "Did I stumble into some kind of fairy tale quest?"

Definitely not an actual Hemsworth...that accent was pure prep school with a touch of New York. Having spent her entire life in close proximity to a NESCAC college gave her an ear for it. Still criminally good looking.

Her pulse slowed. The Twins kept him at the edge of the clearing, conducting a thorough examination of his feet and ankles. If he was a criminal, their prey-animal instincts failed them. The two hens, sisters by choice, might have walked straight out of a Disney animation. Both broad and a little swaybacked with smooth feathers, one palest blue-gray, the other the color of a summer wheat field in an overexposed Ridley Scott dream sequence, they circled the stranger's feet, clucking softly and picking at his shoelaces.

He'd better keep his distance; her masks were all in the house. How could she have anticipated company appearing from out of the woods in the form of a ridiculously attractive hiker?

"You're off the Horizon Trail, if that's where you were walking. This is private property."

He picked a dandelion and offered it to Lavender, who snatched the treat and hopped away, Buffy in her wake. "Lilac Lane?"

Poppy narrowed her eyes at him. Not a totally lost hiker, then.

"Nick Cooper." He started to offer his hand, then remembered and pushed it back into his pocket with an adorably awkward laugh. "I'm renting the Fullers' cabin for...well, for now."

Nicky didn't mention... So that was where Professor McNair was on her way to in that enviable car.

Poppy sighed. Of course *available, age-appropriate* Hemsworth lookalikes didn't wander into her parents' backyard. Mathilda flapped back onto the picnic table, greeting them both with the whirring chirp Poppy thought of as purring. "Poppy Daley. My mother cultivates the lilacs."

Nick grinned, charmed by Mathilda. "And you keep the hens?"

Stung, Poppy snatched up her laptop. "Yes. I keep the hens." She gestured to a nearby hemlock stand. "You can pick up the Horizon Trail about 40 yards that way."

Mustering the small dignity afforded to her by Maybelline Lash Sensational, Poppy spun on her heel and made for the barn, hoping Nick Cooper didn't notice the chicken poop on her flip-flop heel.

"You owe me," Nick said into the phone. "You didn't tell me she was pretty. And not retired. I swallowed not only my foot, but my ankle and most of my shin."

Elisha laughed. "I mistook her for your housekeeper. What makes you think I'm going to be any help?"

"You let me think my retired neighbors were down there, not a woman my age who's probably their daughter."

"I didn't know." She laughed again, musical and unrepentant. "And what can you do? This whole lockdown scenario is less than ideal for romantic gestures."

"Whoa." Nick pulled the phone away from his face for a second, as though Elisha could see his expression. "Who said *romantic*?"

"You called me asking what you could do for your pretty, not-retired neighbor..."

Elisha was often right. Infuriatingly so. She also often had the answers. Infuriatingly.

"Did you make it into the pastry shop in town before all this?" Nick imagined her hand waving in the direction of the window of her airy loft, one of three upscale condos carved out of a barn on a hillside north of the college. *All this...* The unobstructed view of the valley priceless. Nick wondered if her self-quarantine was made easier by the gilded sunsets she watched every night.

She would worry about her grandparents. She would

worry about Ben. But he didn't mention them. "I didn't. Probably should have, huh?"

"Call them and order the lilac woman some chocolate croissants. The owner is delivering orders until she can reopen."

"Let me guess," Nick said. "You two got pedicures together before the salons closed?"

"No. Frankly, she drives me crazy, but her chocolate croissants are a decent alternative to sex."

Nick wasn't sure anything made of flour and butter was quite that good. "Why does the Princess of Pomfret even have a list of alternatives to sex?"

"I hate that nickname." She paused for a long moment. "And I'm not interested in sex right now. Too many complications. Croissants, however, can be forgiven by sufficient running and lifting."

Nick heard her unspoken closing of the topic. "So, I should order a chocolate croissant delivery from that bakery to say I'm sorry to my neighbor." *My very pretty, very much not-retired-matron neighbor who makes keeping chickens very appealing.*

"I'll text you the link. If your lilac girl's the irresponsible type, she'll turn up at your door in sexy lingerie to say thank you."

"She's not my lilac girl—"

But Elisha ended the call. Nick peered out over the forest canopy in the direction of Lilac Lane, unable to unsee the image of Poppy Daley, all those nearly blue-black curls tumbling over soft shoulders, smoldering up at him from beneath long, sooty lashes.

Fantasy Poppy wasn't wearing scraps of satin and lace. Nick found everyday underthings far sexier than delicate, complicated straps and netting. Easier to slide hands under, easier to discard en route to sweet curves and warm flesh.

When Elisha's text disturbed his runaway imagination, Nick clicked the link and called the bakery straightaway. Whether she thanked him or not, he owed Poppy an apology, and he was too practical to leave an imaginary girl outside in the woods in her underwear. She'd get eaten alive.

If it was his fantasy, that was his privilege.

Keep reading at https://books2read.com/TheBestLaidPlans

About the Publisher

Bannerwing Books is a writers' co-op founded in 2012 by Cameron D. Garriepy, and completed by Angela Amman and Mandy Dawson. Currently residing on Slack, somewhere in the ether between Boston, Detroit, and Paso Robles, Bannerwing presents works by Stephanie Ayers, Ericka Clay, and Liz Zimmers, as well as collections featuring Andra Watkins, Kate Shrewsday, and Kameko Murakami.

www.bannerwingbooks.com

facebook.com/bannerwingbooks

twitter.com/bannerwingbooks

Made in the USA
Middletown, DE
24 August 2024